Mommy and the Maverick

Meg Maxwell

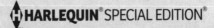

HARLEQUIN® SPECIAL EDITION®

Special thanks and acknowledgment are given to Meg Maxwell for her contribution to the Montana Mavericks: The Great Family Roundup continuity.

Recycling programs
for this product may
not exist in your area.

ISBN-13: 978-0-373-62363-1

Mommy and the Maverick

Copyright © 2017 by Harlequin Books S.A.

This edition published by arrangement with Harlequin Books S.A.

For questions and comments about the quality of this book, please contact us at CustomerService@Harlequin.com.

Printed in U.S.A.

www.Harlequin.com

"What about you, Marissa? What would make you happy?"

"When my crew is happy, I'm happy." She smiled. "I guess it's hard to separate one from the other. It's been a long time since it's been just me, you know?

"What would make me happy?" She paused and looked at him, and she was pretty sure her answer was written all over her face.

He sucked in a breath and leaned close and kissed her. She kissed him back, grateful for their secluded corner.

"Just for tonight," she said.

"Just for tonight."

She kissed him again, her hands on his face, everything she felt going into the fierce kiss. "No strings attached," she whispered.

"That's always been the case," he said.

No strings. She'd shake on that again, but not on being friends. She couldn't be casual friends with Autry, not after this, and certainly not after they made love.

"Maybe we should take this conversation upstairs," he said.

"I think we're done talking," she whispered and kissed him again.

MONTANA MAVERICKS:
The Great Family Roundup—
Real cowboys and real love in Rust Creek Falls!

Dear Reader,

Autry Jones, one of the five famous Jones brothers (famous in *Montana Mavericks* for being millionaire business cowboys!), thinks he's immune to love. He flies into tiny Rust Creek Falls in his private jet to visit his brothers for a few weeks before he'll have to jet off to Paris on family business. A wilderness romance while there would be just fine with him—as long as she's not a single mother. After what Autry went through last year? No single moms. No kids. Never.

Oh, Autry. At a viewing party for *The Great Roundup* at everyone's favorite Rust Creek Falls bar and grill, Ace in the Hole, he falls hard for Marissa Fuller...who he's about to discover is a single mom of not one little girl but *three*. Autry thinks his self-diagnosed immunity to love and kids will keep him from falling for the sweet family for the three weeks he's in town. Even his two brothers in town, Walker and Hudson, shake their heads at him...

I hope you enjoy Marissa and Autry's story! I love hearing from readers and can be reached at authormegmaxwell@gmail.com. And if you didn't already know, Meg Maxwell is my pen name—my real name is Melissa Senate and you can also write me at melissasenate@yahoo.com. Meg is a childhood nickname, so I answer to both.

Happy Reading!

Meg Maxwell

MegMaxwell.com

Meg Maxwell lives on the coast of Maine with her teenage son, their beagle and their black-and-white cat. When she's not writing, Meg is either reading, at the movies or thinking up new story ideas on her favorite little beach (even in winter) just minutes from her house. Interesting fact: Meg Maxwell is a pseudonym for author Melissa Senate, whose women's fiction titles have been published in over twenty-five countries.

Books by Meg Maxwell

Harlequin Special Edition

Hurley's Homestyle Kitchen

A Cowboy in the Kitchen
The Detective's 8 lb, 10 oz Surprise
The Cowboy's Big Family Tree
The Cook's Secret Ingredient
Charm School for Cowboys

In memory of my beloved grandparents.

Chapter One

Autry Jones stood on the sidewalk in front of Just Us Kids Day Care Center, trying to process that his family's corporation, the venerable Jones Holdings, Inc. was in the day care business. And that he was about to walk inside the building.

Autry and children didn't mix. Joneses and children weren't *supposed* to mix, but somehow, two of his four brothers had not only settled down with wives in this small Montana town, but were heavily invested in a day care franchise.

Autry took off his aviator-style sunglasses and tucked them in his pocket. He sucked in a breath and pulled open the front door.

There were babies everywhere.

Well, little humans, Autry amended, as he stepped inside and glanced around the main room. And only a handful of them, now that he actually counted. A big-cheeked baby was in a woman's arms. A toddler wearing a shirt decorated with a cartoon monkey was building a tower of cardboard blocks. A little girl with bright red pigtails sat at a pint-size table, drawing a picture of a house and the sun with a smiley face in the center.

The middle-aged woman holding the baby smiled at him and walked over. He read her name tag: Miss Marley.

"Hi, Miss Marley," he said, extending his hand. "I'm Autry Jones. My—"

The woman grinned and shifted the baby in her arms. "No introductions necessary, Autry. You're Walker and Hudson's brother. I'd know a Jones brother anywhere. They mentioned you were flying in today. But you just missed them. They left for Ace in the Hole. Everyone in town is getting together there for a viewing party."

Ace in the Hole? Was that some kind of golf tournament? He could see Walker on the course, but Hudson? No way. "A viewing party?"

Miss Marley looked at him as if he'd been living on Mars for a while. "To watch *The Great Roundup*, of course! I plucked the short straw, so I'm on duty with this lil cutie and the Myler siblings until their parents get off work, but three people promised to record the premiere for me."

Ah, a TV show, Autry figured. He didn't watch much TV. As president of Jones Holdings, an international company involved in real estate and manufacturing—and lately, a day care franchise—Autry was focused on negotiating deals and making money. Having time to watch TV was beyond him, despite the stretches he spent in airport lounges and on flights to everywhere from Dubai to Australia. Free time was about preparation—which was practically his family's motto. Well, his father's. Not that that had always been the case for Autry. Something he didn't like to think about.

Now, though, Autry had found himself with an entire three weeks, twenty-one days, to himself. No necessary meetings. No deals to broker—not until late August, when he'd have to be in Paris for the Thorpe Corp. negotiations. He could be spending these much-needed vacation weeks on the beach in Bali or southern California. Appreciating the view, including sexy women in bikinis. But two of his brothers had shocked him— and the rest of the Jones family—by settling down with wives in the boondocks of Montana.

Rust Creek Falls. If he looked one way there was a building—barely. Another, Montana wilderness. Walker hadn't been kidding when he referred to Rust Creek Falls as something of the "Wild West."

Speaking of his oldest brother, Walker Jones the Third, who didn't have a speck of small town in him, the company CEO had not only built a Jones Holdings, Inc. office here, but had built an actual log cabin for him and his new wife, Lindsay Dalton Jones, to live in. Autry wouldn't have believed it, but he'd seen the cabin with his own eyes at their wedding, back in May. Granted, it was pure luxury, but still. Logs. A cabin. Montana wilderness. Autry expected that of his brother Hudson, who loved ranch life and the open spaces of Wyoming and Montana. Hudson operated the business of the day care for Walker, and had fallen for the manager, Bella Stockton, and now the happily married couple lived together at the Lazy B Ranch.

Two Jones brothers down. None to go. Well, three, but Autry, despite being thirty-three years old, wasn't the marrying kind, and though he wasn't close with any of his brothers, he couldn't see Gideon and Jensen getting hitched. But if Walker and Hudson had, anything was possible.

He had these three weeks, zero relationships with his brothers and a chance to change that.

There was discord between his father, the domineering, controlling Walker Jones the Second, and his brother Walker the Third; their father had given up years ago on "wayward" Hudson following in the family footsteps. If Autry didn't take this time to try to bond with his brothers a little, maybe smooth over things between them and their father, the family would disintegrate. Unfortunately, his dad didn't seem to care, nor did his mother, so it was up to Autry. Why he cared so much, he wasn't sure. But he did. He wanted to know his brothers. Especially now that they'd done something so…unexpected, like falling in love and getting hitched. Making lifetime commitments.

"Whose daddy are you?" the little red-haired girl asked suddenly, her big eyes on Autry, her crayon poised in the air.

Autry froze. *No one's. And that's the way it's going to stay.* "No, sweetheart, I'm not anyone's daddy. I'm just visiting."

Miss Marley smiled at the girl. "This is Mr. Walker's and Mr. Hudson's brother, Mr. Autry."

"Mr. Walker and Mr. Hudson are nice," the girl said, then went back to coloring.

What? Walker was nice? Hudson has his moments, but Autry wouldn't go so far as to characterize him as nice. What had Rust Creek Falls done to the Jones brothers?

And what had his family done to *him* if he thought the words *nice* and *Jones* could never be paired in the same sentence?

Autry looked around the colorful space with its square foam mats with letters of the alphabet, its bean-bags and rows of cubbies in primary colors. Kid-size tables and chairs dotted the room. He could see door-ways leading into classrooms, a nursery with cribs, and what looked like a break room. The area above the reception desk, with *WELCOME* spelled out in blocks, was full of photographs of babies and watercolors by "Sophia, age three" and "Marcus, age seven"

How his brothers spent so much time around kids, Autry had no idea. Autry liked kids just fine. As long as he wasn't having them or raising them. In fact, Autry had a rule for himself when it came to dating: no women with baby fever. And under no circumstances would he date a single mother.

Lulu's sweet face came to mind. A face he hadn't let himself think about in months. Another big-cheeked baby, but with silky dark hair. Lulu, short for Louisa, had been a package deal with her single mother, beau-tiful Karinna. Autry had fallen in love with Karinna and soon felt like Lulu was his own flesh and blood. Suddenly the jet-setter had been changing diapers and wanting to stay in and listen to the woman he loved sing lullabies, instead of disappearing for weeks at a time on Jones Holdings business. But a few months later, when she left him for someone even richer, Autry lost not only his heart but the child he'd come to love.

So single mothers: never again.

"Ace in the Hole is on Sawmill Street," Miss Marley said, interrupting his thoughts. "Just past the gas station. Can't miss it. Oh, and order the ribs. Trust me. Best in town."

Ah. Ace in the Hole was starting to sound like a bar and grill. The kind with a big screen TV. Ribs and a good craft beer sounded pretty good. Plus, he was looking forward to seeing his brothers and getting to know their wives. Autry had flown in for the weddings, but had had to leave the next day. Now, he had weeks to solve the mystery of his brothers' complete turnarounds.

"Thanks for letting me know, Miss Marley," Autry said. "I'll be sure to order the ribs."

"Go, Brenna and Travis!" Marley said, giving the baby a little pump in the air. "Imagine that, two of our own on a reality TV show. So exciting!"

Autry had no idea who Brenna and Travis were, but a reality TV show called *The Great Roundup* probably had something to do with cattle. Maybe horses?

"Da," said the baby in Miss Marley's grasp, reaching out his arms toward Autry.

An old ache gripped Autry, catching him off guard. He'd thought he was done with the sudden stabbing pain over what had happened.

Marley smiled. "That's not your daddy, Dylan, but yes, he does look like your father with his blond hair and blue eyes."

Autry forced a smile. "It was nice to meet you," he said, extending his hand, then he headed out the door.

The one thing you could count on in this life was that there would be no babies or children in a bar.

Ace in the Hole, here I come. And not a minute too soon.

* * *

"Wow," Marissa Fuller said as she and her nine-year-old daughter, Abby, walked into the Ace in the Hole. "Standing room only tonight." Good thing she'd decided to leave her two younger daughters at home with their grandparents.

Abby's face lit up. "This is so exciting, Mom! The first episode of *The Great Roundup* is *finally* going to be on TV! Did you ever think a reality TV show would film right here in Rust Creek Falls? I could totally pass out from the anticipation! All those cute cowboys competing in teams for a zillion dollars—in Western feats and wilderness survival…and two who we actually know! I can't wait to find Janie and watch!"

How her daughter got that all out in one breath, Marissa would never know. While Abby scanned the crowd for her best friend, Marissa looked around for two empty seats. There was *one*—right next to her good friend Anne Lattimore, Janie's mother.

"Marissa!" Anne called, waving her over. "I've been saving you this seat for twenty minutes and have gotten a bunch of mean looks by folks who want it. One guy even offered to buy me the sirloin special if I let him have the chair."

"Was he cute?" Abby asked as they approached. "Blond or dark haired? Did he have dimples like Lyle in 2LOVEU?"

Marissa smiled and shook her head, then gratefully sat down next to Anne at the table for two that was wedged between two others. Her daughter's favorite subject was 2LOVEU, a boy band she listened to on repeat for hours. Marissa had heard the songs so often they'd grown on her, too.

"He was cute," Anne told Abby. "But around fifty. And no dimples, sorry."

"Abby, you can sit on my lap, like old times," Marissa said, squeezing her daughter's hand.

Abby's eyes widened. "Mom, I'm *nine*," she whispered in horror.

"No worries," Anne said, smiling at Abby. "Janie's over there, sitting on the floor in the kids section. She saved you a spot, too."

"Bye!" Abby squealed and ran over to the area, where Marissa could see around thirty or so children sitting on foam mats, talking excitedly and munching on the free popcorn the Ace staff was handing out in brown paper bags. There was a good view of the two giant screen televisions on stands on either side of the bar. No matter where you sat in the room, you could see them.

"You're the best, Anne," Marissa said, scooting a bit closer to her friend to avoid being elbowed in the ribs by the woman at the next table. A divorced mom with a full-time job as a receptionist at the veterinarian's office, Anne had her hands full but her act completely together. Something Marissa was working on. "I meant to get here twenty minutes ago, but Kiera couldn't find her favorite doll and had the tantrum of all tantrums just as I was leaving. I thought tantrums were supposed to stop by five years old."

Anne smiled, pushing a swath of her wavy blond hair behind her ear. "One of my neighbors threw a tantrum this morning over someone's dog walking on the edge of her property. I don't think there's an age limit, sorry."

Marissa laughed. "And then Kaylee managed to

smush a green bean in her ear at dinner, so I had to deal with a three-year-old sobbing that this means she's going to turn into a green bean."

Anne squeezed Marissa's hand. "Oh, to be three years old."

But finally, Marissa had made it. Her mom and dad, doting grandparents, had shooed her out the door, assuring her they'd help Kiera find the doll, and calm down Kaylee. But even when Marissa needed a night out so badly she could scream, she never felt comfortable leaving her parents to deal with sobs and tantrums. That was Marissa's job. She was the parent. She was the *only* parent.

She may have moved back in with her folks for the sake of the girls—and yes, her sake, too. But she wasn't about to take advantage of her parents' kindness and generosity. They'd been there for her two years ago when her husband, Mike, had died. They'd been there when she was struggling to make ends meet. They'd been there when she'd surrendered to the notion that she needed help, and had accepted their offer to move home. But her three daughters were *her* responsibility, and no matter how tired she was from her job at the sheriff's office, or comforting a sick child at three in the morning, Marissa was their mom. Despite that, though, living under her parents' roof sometimes made her feel like one of the kids instead of a twenty-seven-year-old widow, a grown-up.

A cheer went up in the room and Marissa glanced at the TV. It was showing a teaser promo for *The Great Roundup*, which was about to start in a few minutes, and there was Brenna O'Reilly, hometown girl, giving an interview, reality-TV-style, to someone off camera about how she never thought she could do this, but here she was, a hairstylist from Rust Creek Falls, participating in the competition with her hot fiancé, and she was going to give it her all.

You go, Brenna. Marissa knew all about finding herself in uncharted territory. You gave it your all or... There was actually no alternative.

"Brenna O'Reilly and Travis Dalton?" Anne said. She smiled and shook her head. "The cowboy no one ever thought would settle down and the flirty hairstylist always up for adventure—engaged. Crazy."

Marissa had gone to high school with Brenna, who'd been a year behind her. They'd been only acquaintances, but she had to agree. Plus, hadn't Brenna always talked about getting out of Rust Creek Falls? Granted, she had for the TV show, which had filmed for what must have been six very exciting weeks at the High Lonesome Guest Ranch. Rumor had it that Brenna and Travis would be coming to the viewing party, even though they'd been invited to watch the first episode with the producers and some of the other competitors.

"Chemistry works in mysterious ways," Jamie Stockton said, his arm around his wife, Fallon O'Reilly Stockton—Brenna's sister.

It sure was nice to see Jamie Stockton out for a change. Before he'd fallen in love with Fallon, the widowed rancher had been raising his baby triplets on his own. If anyone needed a night out, it was Jamie.

Fallon smiled and nodded, raising her beer mug. She had visited her sister on location during the filming of the show last month. But Fallon wouldn't say a word about what had gone on behind the scenes. Apparently, she'd had to sign confidentiality papers not to ruin any surprises.

What the whole town did know was that originally, Travis, the ultimate showman cowboy, was the only Rust Creek Falls contestant on the show, which was about cowboys—men and women—competing in Western-style challenges. But when the producers were in town last month to film some hometown segments and saw what amazing chemistry Travis had with his girlfriend, Brenna—and how camera ready Brenna was—they'd invited them both on the show. No one had even suspected Travis and Brenna were dating, but the next thing everyone knew, Travis had proposed and they were competing as *The Great Roundup*'s "engaged couple." If Marissa could binge watch the whole season in one night, she would. But she, like everyone else, would have to wait for every episode over the next several months.

"Now, that sounds like Travis," said Nate Crawford, who owned the general store and a hotel in town, "Asking a woman to marry him for good ratings." He grinned and shook his head. ·

Anne laughed. "I saw them a bunch of times together last month during the filming here. When the cameras weren't rolling. No way were they faking anything for ratings. Those two are in love for sure."

"Still, I can't imagine proposing to a woman on a whim," Zach Dalton said, adjusting his bolo tie as though it were squeezing his neck. Marissa glanced at Zach at the table on their other side. The handsome newcomer to town and his four brothers were cousins of Travis's.

"Well, no matter what happened behind the scenes,"

Anne said, "everything sure worked out for Travis and Brenna. They're engaged."

Marissa sighed. It sure had. All the romance in the air had left her a little wistful. Last month, her daughter Abby had talked nonstop about how "dreamy" their new town "star" Travis was, almost as dreamy as Lyle, the lead singer of 2LOVEU. And Marissa had always admired Brenna's free-spirited ways, especially back in high school. Brenna had had lots of dates, while Marissa had dated only one boy throughout high school and always expected they would get married. When she got pregnant after prom night, she'd married Michael Fuller at age eighteen. But Brenna had sown her wild oats and found love when she was ready for it. *Good for you, Brenna.*

Just as Marissa was about to try to flag one of the very busy waitresses, who were all racing around with platters of steaks and appetizers and ribs and trays of beer and soda, Abby ran over.

"Mom!" her daughter said, her brown eyes all dreamy. "That's the one you should pick. For sure."

Pick? Huh? Marissa looked in the direction her daughter was staring.

Ah. Three very good-looking men—two the Jones brothers and a third, who looked just like them— stood at the bar, talking, smiling, whispering. Marissa couldn't take her eyes off the one she didn't know. She was pretty sure she'd heard that Walker and Hudson, who owned Just Us Kids, had other brothers. And the tall Adonis between them, with his thick dark blond hair and sparkling, intense blue eyes, his designer shirt clearly costing more than her three kids' wardrobes for a year, had to be a Jones. They were millionaires, yes, but also rare men who looked like they belonged both in Montana and a big city. There was something about the cut of the Western shirt, the premium leather cowboy boots, the belt buckle on which was carved the initials AJ and the trim fit of low-slung dark jeans. Since her daughter knew who Walker and Hudson were, the girl had to be talking about the one in the middle. Abby was right. He was sexy.

"They look like they should be in an ad for men's cologne," Marissa quipped. "Or on a movie poster. But pick for what?" she asked her daughter.

Abby grinned and leaned close. "To be your boyfriend." The girl giggled and ran back to her seat next to her best friend.

Anne burst into laughter, but Marissa sighed. This was not the first time Abby had brought up the *b* word.

"Isn't she a little young to be this boy crazy?" Marissa asked her friend. "I mean, it's one thing for Abby to be putting up posters of 2LOVEU on her bedroom wall. It's another for her to be sizing up every man she sees as a potential love interest for her own mother."

Anne smiled but sighed, too. "Janie's the same. I hear her say good-night to the lead singer of 2LOVEU before bed. We weren't much different with our posters when we were kids."

"Except we can't remember being kids because we're a hundred years old," Marissa pointed out.

Anne laughed. "Exactly."

Marissa found herself staring at the gorgeous stranger again. She had to hand it to her daughter—the girl had amazing taste. Marissa loved the way his blond hair swooped up and back like a Hemsworth brother's. The few crinkles at the edges of his

blue eyes suggested he was a bit older than her. Early
thirties, she'd say. And those shoulders. Those arms.
The way his waist narrowed down to those delicious
jeans, which—

Oh my God.

He raised his beer glass at her and winked.

He'd caught her staring!

Mortifying!

"Can the floor open up and swallow me?" Marissa
said, wishing the woman at the table in front of her had
bigger hair so she could block Marissa and her cheeks,
which had to be bright red.

"And miss the start of *The Great Roundup*?" Anne
said with an evil grin. "Go talk to him! Hurry. You
only have a few minutes."

"What? Talk to *that*? That absolute gorgeous speci-
men of man? He barely looks real he's so hot."

Anne laughed. "The waitresses are so busy we'll
never get served before the show starts. Go get us two
drafts and order a platter of something yummy. Perfect
excuse to meet His Hotness. I heard Lindsay mention
that her brother-in-law Autry was due in town this week
and that Autry has been to just about every country in
the world. How exciting is that? The man is a jet-setter.
And gorgeous. Go get him."

A tiny bit of Marissa, who was trying to be more
"in the moment," per a magazine article, wanted to
do just that.

But come on. Marissa was a widowed mother of
three young daughters and living with her parents. She
might seem attractive across a room when he knew
nothing about her, but she had no doubt that the man
would run all the way back to Tulsa, where she'd heard

the Jones brothers hailed from, the moment he discovered what her life was.

"I can just see that very expensive-looking man plucking green beans out of Kiera's ears," Marissa said. "*Not.* He's nice to look at, but come on. I'm going to be on my own until Kaylee's out of high school." Which was only, *gulp*, fifteen more years.

"Marissa Fuller!" Anne chastised her with a smile. "What did Brenna and Travis's crazy whirlwind romance teach us? That you just never know. If you're open to it, if you're *there*, love just might show up."

Marisa was so touched by how positive Anne always was—and Anne was the divorcee who'd never, ever gotten over her first love, Daniel Stockton. She wrapped her friend in a hug. "Maybe we'll both find love again," Marissa said.

"Well, if I were you, I'd march over to the bar before some other single woman does."

But Marissa stayed put, an eye on Abby and her thoughts back home. Yes, a night out was sorely needed, but Marissa missed putting her little ones to bed and wishing them sweet dreams. That was her life. Not hot men in thousand-dollar cowboy boots.

But this particular one sure was nice to fantasize about.

Chapter Two

Autry watched the brunette with the dark eyes try to snag the waitress's attention at least five times. She wasn't having any luck. Which gave him his perfect in. He asked the bartender for two of the finest craft beers and got an eye roll and two drafts on tap.

"I keep telling you, Autry," his brother Walker said. "This is Rust Creek Falls. And a dive bar *in* Rust Creek Falls. We don't do twelve-dollar bottles of beer here." His brother's wedding band glinted in the dim lighting.

"And *two* beers?" Hudson asked with a grin. "You got here, what? Five minutes ago? And you already have your eye on someone?"

Autry smiled. "I'm in town for three weeks. That's a long time. And you two have wives now and lives outside Jones Holdings. I need something to fill the hours."

"Careful, brother," Walker said, running a hand

through his dirty-blond hair. "There's something in the water here. It got me. It got Hudson. It's gonna get you."

"Not a chance," Autry said, his gaze on the luscious brunette beauty. Had a woman in jean shorts and a yellow T-shirt ever been so stunning? "End of August, I'll be in Paris. As single as ever."

"If you say so," Hudson said, raising his beer glass at Autry.

Autry caught the smirk Hudson gave Walker. No matter what, it sure was nice to see Walker and Hudson together. Joking, laughing, sharing a beer. Once, back when they were all kids, Walker and Hudson had been close. But they hadn't been for years. Looked like being neighbors had changed that some.

A woman standing next to them with a baby in her arms turned to Walker. "Hey, Walker, will you hold Jackson for me for a moment while I go hug my aunt and uncle?"

"You bet, Candace," Walker said, taking the baby as if he did this sort of thing all the time.

Walker Jones. The Third. With a baby in his arms. Bouncing it a bit and making baby talk. "Who's a cute one?" Walker said, nuzzling his nose at the tiny tot.

Good Lord. What planet was Autry on? Was Rust Creek Falls in another dimension?

And there really were babies everywhere. Even in bars. Though, granted, tonight was a special occasion. From the looks of the place, the entire town had turned up to watch *The Great Roundup*. With all the buzz Autry had heard about the show in the ten minutes he'd been in the Ace in the Hole, he was excited to watch. Cowboys competing for a million bucks? Hell yeah. That was his kind of TV. The Jones family might be

millionaires, but they were cowboys at heart. Autry's
first memory was of being on the back of a horse. And
the first gift he'd ever gotten? A "piggy" bank in the
shape of a stallion. Money and horses were two hall-
marks of the Jones family.

The baby's mother returned and held out her arms
for little Jackson. "You're a peach," she said to Walker.

Walker, a peach? Autry couldn't help himself. He
laughed.

Hudson grinned. "Trust me. If peachhood got
Walker and me, you're next. You're here."

"I'm immune," Autry said.

"*Sure*, bro," Hudson said with a knowing nod. He
glanced toward the tables. "Bella's waving us over to
our seats. Our rib platters arrived."

Autry glanced at their table—two entire tables away
from the brunette beauty. Way too far.

"Let's all go sit down," Walker said, nodding at his
wife, Lindsay, who sat next to Bella. "I'm really glad
you're here, Autry. We barely got to talk at the weddings. After the show we'll all head over to Maverick
Manor for a nightcap." Walker clapped Autry on the
shoulder, then followed Hudson across the room.

The bartender placed the two beers Autry had ordered on the bar. "Be right there," Autry called.

Beers in hand, he wove his way through tables and
the standing room–only crowd. There was no way in
hell he could resist meeting this woman. Just as there
was no chance in that same hell they'd have anything
other than a few amazing weeks together before he jet-
ted off to Paris. If she was game, what was the harm
in letting something happen between them for twenty-
one delicious days? And something *would* happen. The

closer he got to her table, the more her brown eyes and her unenhanced pink-red lips drew him in. He had to know her. Well, on a superficial level.

"Hello," he said, nodding at the brunette and the blonde beside her. "Here you go," he said, handing a beer to each woman. "Autry Jones, at your service."

"I knew you had to be a Jones brother," the brunette said. "I'm Marissa Fuller and this is my friend Anne Lattimore. Thanks for the beers. That was very thoughtful." She smiled and took a sip, then set down the glass and looked around. Not at him.

Huh. Where was the flirtatiousness? Where was the fawning? Where was the sidling up to him and pressing herself against him like most women did?

"Are you in town visiting your brothers?" Marissa asked, taking another sip of beer.

He nodded. "For three weeks. I'm used to Tulsa, so Rust Creek Falls is a nice change."

"Are you staying with Walker or Hudson?" Marissa asked. "I'll admit, sometimes I drive by Walker's house just to look at it. It's amazing. A mansion made entirely out of logs."

He smiled. "A log mansion for Walker and a beautiful ranch for Hudson. I visited both homes after their weddings back in May and June. But I'm staying at Maverick Manor."

Surprise crossed her pretty features. "For three weeks?"

"I like room service," he said. The truth was that he wasn't close enough with either brother to feel comfortable staying with them that long. And he did like room service. Besides, Autry had gotten so used to luxury hotels that anything too homespun would feel…wrong and claustrophobic.

She laughed. "Don't we all."

Her smile had him so captivated he almost forgot where he was. But then the lights dimmed and he noticed Walker waving him over. "Autry, I'm gonna eat your share of the ribs," his brother called.

Marissa glanced at Walker and laughed. "Better get over there before there's nothing but a plate of bones."

"Nice to meet you, Autry," Anne said. "And thanks for the beer."

He. Could. Not. Make. His. Legs. Move. Away.

"Uh, buddy, you're blocking my view of the TV," a man said, and Autry snapped back to attention.

"Sorry," he said to the guy. He smiled at Marissa and her friend and headed over to his seat.

Autry glanced back at Marissa shortly after, but instead of ogling him with a sexy look on her face, letting him know she was up for meeting later, she was chatting with her friend.

Well, well, he thought, biting into a succulent rib with the best barbecue sauce he'd had in years. A challenge had just presented itself. And *challenge* was Autry Jones's middle name.

Hmm, Marissa thought as the credits began rolling on the two big-screen TVs. The man was in town for three weeks. Might be nice to go out to dinner or a movie with a very good-looking man, a nice change of pace from watching *ET* and *Frozen* for the thirtieth time in her parents' family room, then cleaning up errant popcorn kernels.

"There's Travis!" Anne said, as the cowboy's handsome face filled the screen. They were showing a promo video he'd shot last month in Rust Creek Falls, talking about his love of horses and his fiancée. Then there was Travis and Brenna on horseback, riding along with the other contestants to the "canteen" where the host, Jasper Ridge, a middle-aged cowboy all in black with a black handlebar mustache, awaited. The Ace in the Hole erupted in cheers.

Jasper explained the rules—the last cowboy or cowgirl standing would win one million dollars. *Whoa boy.* That was a lot of money. The contestants would be paired for some challenges, but each was competing on his or her own. So alliances could be made, but it might not get the contestants anywhere but tricked and eliminated. Marissa watched as the twenty-two contestants were introduced in little snippets. There was the Franklin family—widowed Fred and his twin sons, Rob and Joey. A grizzled cowboy named Wally Wilson in his late sixties. A fortysomething divorcée named Roberta and a handsome former soldier, Steve, with a prosthetic leg. Marissa's attention was snagged by one contestant in particular—a sexy blonde rodeo star named Summer Knight.

From just the first five minutes it was clear to Marissa that Summer had a huge crush on Travis. She kept trying to sidle up to him, but Brenna, never one to sit quietly by, sidled right up between them, nudging Summer away. Marissa had to smile. And it was clear that the divorcée, Roberta, was very interested in the war hero, who was at least a decade younger. From the way Steve looked at Roberta, the man was smitten with her, too.

The host, Jasper, explained how the main challenges

would work—contestants would be paired in teams and the events would involve everything from building a lean-to to cow roping to hay-bale racing. The winning contestant in each challenge would receive immunity for the next one, and after the day, one contestant would be eliminated.

Marissa sipped her beer while the contestants made "immunity" bracelets of braided leather and beads and put them in a carved wooden box with much ceremony. Then the group set up a tent camp and built a community fire in front. Finally it was time for the first challenge, freeze branding cattle, and Travis and Brenna were paired together. When neither was eliminated at the end of the episode, everyone cheered.

Suddenly an even bigger cheer erupted in the bar, folks standing and clapping. The Ace in the Hole was so crowded that Marissa couldn't see what was going on. She turned to Anne. "What are we missing?"

Anne shrugged, and they both glanced around. A crowd had formed by the door. Marissa craned her neck. She could just make out a pink cowboy hat. Marissa knew of only one woman who wore a pink hat.

"It's Brenna and Travis!" someone shouted.

As word spread across the Ace in the Hole that the hometown stars had shown up, everyone started clapping and wolf whistling.

"Hot wings and a round for everyone!" Travis called out. "On me."

"Lemonade for the kids!" Brenna added with a grin.

The cheers got even louder as the waitresses headed into the kitchen to make good on Travis's generosity.

"Thank you all so much for coming to cheer us on," Travis said, lifting his Stetson.

"Ya'll *were* cheering for us, right?" Brenna added with a grin.

Marissa didn't have a good view of the pair, but she could see Brenna's long red hair in a loose braid under the pink cowboy hat. Handsome Travis was in jeans and boots, his arm slung over Brenna's shoulder.

And glinting on Brenna's finger was a diamond engagement ring.

As Brenna and Travis answered questions about the episode, careful not to give away anything about episode two, Marissa couldn't help but notice the way the pair looked at each other as each spoke. They were truly in love. Travis gazed at Brenna with such warmth and respect in his eyes. And Brenna had never looked so happy.

Good for them, Marissa thought. Feeling just slightly jealous. In a good way. Maybe being a little envious meant that one day she'd want that for herself.

Of course, she couldn't imagine having some big romance. She was a widowed mother of three young children. That was her life. That was her full-time job, despite her part-time job at the sheriff's office. How on earth could she even have time for a hot love affair?

"Love is in the air in Rust Creek Falls," Anne whispered. "If it happened to them, it could happen to us."

Marissa watched as Travis dipped Brenna for a dramatic kiss, covering their faces with his cowboy hat. Sigh. Had she ever been kissed like that? Even in the brief window when she and Mike had been just a couple and not parents?

"Please," Marissa said. "They're TV stars. I'm just regular old me in my jean shorts."

"Well, someone who's anyone but 'regular old me'

sure seems to like those jean shorts," Anne said, wiggling her eyebrows with a sneaky grin.

"What?" Marissa asked but her gaze slid over toward where Autry Jones was sitting.

He was looking right at her, his expression a mix of warm, friendly and downright...flirtatious.

He raised his glass to her and she smiled, then turned back to the TV. She took another peek, and Autry was deep in conversation with his brother Hudson.

Well, here's your chance to be a little more adventurous, Marissa told herself, admiring the way his hunter green shirt fit over his broad shoulders. *If the man asks you out, you will say yes. It's just a date. He doesn't have to want to marry you. He doesn't have to want to be father to your kids. You're not looking to get married again, anyway. It's just dinner and a stroll or a movie, culminating, hopefully, in an amazing kiss. Times twenty-one days*, she added. Yes. She decided it right then and there. If Autry asked her out, she'd accept.

But then she glanced up at the sight of Brenna on TV in an ad for next week's episode, her diamond engagement ring sparkling, talking about how gallant and romantic Travis was even while freeze branding cattle. There was no way a man like Autry—single, as far as she knew; childless, as far as she knew; jet-setter, as far as Anne knew—would want to date a widow with three kids, a demanding part-time job, and parents with eagle eyes and a comment about everything.

Sure was nice to think about, though.

Well, so much for sticking around the Ace in the Hole to squeeze through the crowd to congratulate

Brenna or be tapped on the shoulder by that inhumanly hot Autry Jones and asked out on a date.

Not five minutes after the episode officially ended and the television channels were changed to sports analyses, Marissa's mother had called. Kiera was convinced there was a monster in her closet and a half hour of trying to make the five-year-old believe otherwise had only exhausted Marissa's parents. She'd said goodbye to Anne, who was ready to leave herself anyway, and headed home with Abby, who'd talked nonstop on the way about how dreamy Travis was and wasn't it amazing that he was as dreamy on TV as he was in person and it only proved that Lyle from 2LOVEU was probably a regular nice guy in real life just like Travis was.

Marissa was grateful for the chatterbox beside her as they headed into the house. The more Abby talked and required nods and "Oh yes, I agree" from her mother, the less Marissa could think about a certain six-foot-plus, muscular, gorgeous blond man.

She hadn't been able to catch his eye as she'd left. All for the best.

And so Marissa had gone upstairs with her monster-blaster super sprayer, which doubled as her spray bottle of water for fixing her hair and ironing clothes. Roberta Rafferty had tried the monster blaster, but apparently only Mommy had the superpower of vanquishing the monster in the closet.

Armed with the spray bottle, Marissa burst into her daughters' room, tiptoeing so as not to wake Kaylee, who'd managed to sleep through Kiera's tears and Grandma and Grandpa's attempts to prove there was no monster.

"Mommy! The monster is going to get me," Kiera said, holding her pillow in front of her as a shield between herself and the closet on the other side of the room.

Marissa sat down on her middle daughter's bed. "Sweets, I'm your mother and I'll always tell you the truth, no matter what. I promise you that even though you believe there's a monster in the closet, there really isn't. Sometimes our minds tell us something and scare us, even though it's not true."

Kiera tilted her head. "But I saw him! He opened the door and made a mean face at me! He had three eyes!"

"Well, let's see," Marissa said. With Kiera biting her lip and looking nervous, holding out her shield-pillow, Marissa walked over the closet. She opened the door. No monster. Just a lot of pink and purple clothing. "There's no monster, Kiera. I promise."

"Can you spray inside just to be safe?"

Marissa pumped the water bottle, the fine mist landing on the girls' suitcases.

Marissa closed the door and walked back over to Kiera's bed. "There will never be a monster in that closet. You can count on that."

"I feel better now, Mommy."

Three seconds later, Kiera was snoring, her arm wrapped around her stuffed orange monkey. Meanwhile, her mother was completely exhausted.

"You're such a great mom," came a little whisper.

Marissa whirled around.

Her nine-year-old daughter stood in the doorway, looking like she might cry.

"Abby? Are you all right?"

"Yeah. I'm just—"

"What?" Marissa asked, her heart squeezing.

"I'm really glad you're our mom. You always know what to say and do."

Marissa held out her arms and Abby rushed over. Sometimes she forgot that Abby was just nine, right in the middle of kidhood. She was the eldest Fuller girl and took her role as big sister seriously.

"Thank you, Abby," Marissa said. "I love you to the moon and back."

"Me, too, Mom." With that, Abby got into bed. She said good-night to her poster of 2LOVEU above her bed, then grabbed her own favorite stuffed teddy bear that her father had given her when she was born. Within five minutes, Abby was fast asleep.

Marissa watched her daughter's chest rise and fall and pulled up the pink comforter, then kissed her cheek and tiptoed over to Kiera to do the same. Kaylee was on her tummy in her big-girl toddler bed. Marissa bent over to kiss her forehead, then sat down on Abby's desk chair and looked at her girls.

This was her life. And this was everything. Yeah, it might be nice to fantasize about having the attention of a handsome man. A hot man. A gazillionaire, no less. Pure fantasy.

Marissa Fuller had everything she needed and wanted right in this room. Her heart was full and her life was blessed, despite the hardships.

Her head screwed on straight, she got up, said good-night to her parents and thanked them both again for watching the girls while she'd enjoyed a night out with Abby, then went into her bedroom and changed into a T-shirt and yoga pants and finally slid into bed.

Where she immediately thought of Autry Jones.

What it would be like to kiss him. To feel his hands on her.

She smiled. Just a fantasy. Nothing wrong with that, right? Their paths would likely not cross while he was in town. Her life was here and work and grocery shopping and taking the girls to the doughnut shop for an occasional treat.

But again, no reason she couldn't dream about a TV-style romance with Autry Jones in the privacy of her own bedroom.

Chapter Three

"Kaylee, no!" Marissa called, but it was too late. Her three-year-old had pushed her little doll stroller, with a yellow rabbit tucked safely inside, into a huge display of cereal boxes in Crawford's General Store. They came tumbling down, narrowly missing her.

"Oopsies," Kaylee said, her face crumbling. "Sorry." The girl hung her head, tears dripping down her cheeks.

Oh God, Marissa thought, shaking her head. After waking up twice during the night to comfort Kaylee, who had a tooth coming in, she'd had a crazed morning looking for Kiera's other red light-up sneaker and then Abby's favorite shirt, which had "disappeared" from the folded-laundry basket—it turned out it was never put in the hamper. That was followed by a three-hour shift at the reception desk of the sheriff's office, ending with getting yelled at by Anne Lattimore's neighbor for not sending an officer to deal with the dog-being-allowed-to-walk-on-the-edge-of-my-lawn-issue. Marissa didn't need one more thing. But here it was. And it was only eleven in the morning.

"Kaylee, it's—"

She swallowed her *okay* as the girl ran sobbing down the aisle, running so fast that Marissa had to abandon her cart and leap over the boxes of Oat Yummies littering the floor.

"Ah!" Kaylee said. "A giant!"

Marissa dodged a few more cereal boxes and glanced up into the amazing blue eyes of Autry Jones.

The man she'd been unable to stop thinking about. After soothing Kaylee back to sleep last night, Marissa had been so tired she'd squeezed beside her on the toddler bed, imagining Autry's long, lean, muscular physique beside her before she'd finally drifted off to sleep.

"Oh, thank God," Marissa said. "She sure is fast. A human roadblock was just what was needed."

Autry laughed. "Should we find the runaway train's mother before another display of cereal boxes comes tumbling down, this time on top of us?"

Marissa tilted her head. Was it strange that he didn't assume the little getaway artist was hers? "You're looking at her. She pushed her doll stroller a smidge too far and that was that. This is Kaylee. She's three going on ready for the Olympics."

Kaylee continued to stare up at "the giant." Marissa was five feet six and a huge supporter of comfy flat shoes, and Autry towered over her at at least six foot two, so she could understand why Kaylee thought she was dealing with a fairy-tale giant. He was much better looking than giants usually were, though.

"Yours?" Autry said, staring at Marissa.

"Are you a giant?" Kaylee asked, craning her neck.

Autry knelt down in front of the girl. "Nope. I'm an Autry. Autry Jones. And it's very nice to meet you, Kaylee. You know, when I was a kid, I would race my brothers up and down the aisles of supermarkets until the manager marched over to yell at us."

Kaylee tilted her head, understanding only about half of that. "Did you win?"

"I won every now and then," Autry said. "But with four brothers and me right in the middle, there was always one bigger and faster or lighter and faster."

"No fair," Kaylee said. "Guess where we're going now."

"Grocery shopping?" Autry asked.

"But guess why we're here," she said.

"To buy groceries?" Autry suggested, covering his mouth so he wouldn't laugh.

"We're getting picnic stuff," Kaylee said. "Sandwiches and fruit and cookies. You can come, too."

Marissa watched Autry stiffen. Yup, there it was. He now knew she was a mother, likely figured she was divorced or widowed and so had taken a literal and figurative step back.

"Sweetie," she said to her daughter, "Autry is in town to visit his family and I'm sure he has plans for the day." Marissa waited for him to jump on the out she'd just given him.

"What kind of sandwiches?" he asked Kaylee, still kneeling beside her.

"Peanut butter and jelly—my favorite," the girl said.

Autry smiled. "That's my favorite, too. I'd love to come. I have two hours before I have to meet my brothers at my hotel."

Marissa stared at the man. Did he just say he'd love

to come? That peanut butter and jelly sandwiches were his favorite?

Huh.

"Yay!" Kaylee said.

A millionaire executive cowboy was coming to their picnic. Why did Marissa have the feeling this would not be the first time Autry Jones would surprise her?

Whoa boy. What the hell was he doing? When Marissa had told him the cute little girl was hers, for a split second Autry had almost gone running out of the grocery store. No single mothers. That was his rule. And he didn't have many rules. But instead of racing out the door, he'd said yes to going on a family outing. And that was after Marissa had given him a perfect and easy out.

So why hadn't he taken it?

Because he'd been unable to stop thinking about Marissa Fuller since he'd first laid eyes on her yesterday at the Ace in the Hole. He'd been hoping to talk to her after *The Great Roundup* ended, but by the time he'd woven his way through the crowd, she was gone. He and his brothers had met up at his hotel and they'd talked for a while over good scotch in the lobby bar. He'd wanted to ask Walker and Hudson if they knew Marissa, and surely they did, since Rust Creek Falls was such a small town. But Autry realized he didn't want to hear anything about her secondhand; he wanted to get to know her himself.

You can still run, he told himself as he carried the grocery bags containing their picnic and walked alongside Marissa, who held her little girl's hand. They were on their way to a park Marissa had mentioned that was just a bit farther down Cedar Street. He could make up a forgotten appointment. Someone to see. And book the hell away.

But he kept walking, charmed—against his will—by cute Kaylee's light-up sneakers and the way she talked about the puppy that stole her sandwich the last time she went on a picnic with her mom.

"Well, this time, I'll guard your sandwich from every puppy in the park," Autry said.

He felt Marissa's eyes on him. Assessing him? Wondering if he was father material? He wasn't. He was in town temporarily, end of story. As long as he kept his guard up, his wits about him and his eye on the prize, which was to drink in the loveliness of Marissa Fuller for a few weeks, he'd be A-OK.

He glanced at Marissa, surprised again at how damned alluring she was. The woman wore jean shorts, a short-sleeve blue-and-yellow-plaid button-down shirt and orange flip-flops decorated with seashells. Her toenails were each polished a different sparkly color, and something told him she'd let Kaylee give her the pedicure. She wasn't wearing a stitch of makeup, and her wavy, long dark hair fell past her shoulders. She was as opposite the usual woman who caught his eye as possible. Autry met most of the women he dated in airport VIP lounges, alerted to their presence by their click of polished high heels on the floor and the smell of expensive perfume.

"Guess how many sisters I have?" Kaylee asked him, holding her free hand behind her back.

Autry froze. There were more?

"One?" he asked, trying not to visibly swallow.

Kaylee shook her head and giggled.

She let go of Marissa and held out both hands, palms facing him. Ten? She had ten sisters? He was going on a picnic with a mother of eleven?

Earth to Autry, he ordered himself. *The girl is three. Calm down.*

Kaylee giggled again and held up two fingers like a peace sign.

There was nothing peaceful about this. He might not be dating a mother of eleven, but he was dating a mother of three. Not that an impromptu picnic counted as a date. This was just a friendly little picnic. After all, three-year-olds didn't accompany their mothers on first dates.

Autry felt better. Not a date. Just a peanut butter and jelly sandwich and some fruit.

Still, he pulled at the collar of his polo shirt. It was strangling him. And granted, it was August, but was it a thousand degrees suddenly?

"There's the park," Marissa said, pointing down North Buckskin Road.

Autry glanced at the sign as they passed it. Rust Creek Falls Park. He didn't spend a lot of time in parks or going on picnics. But it was eighty-one degrees and sunny, with a delicious breeze that every now and then blew back Marissa's wavy hair, exposing her enticing neck. Perfect park weather. And it wasn't very crowded. A few people walked dogs, a couple joggers ran on the path and a group of teenagers were sunbathing and giggling in the distance.

"Here's a perfect spot," Marissa said. "Right under a shade tree."

"Hi, Mr. Autry," Kaylee said, for absolutely no reason as she stared up at him. *Gulp.* She was looking at him with pure adoration in her twinkly brown eyes. She slipped her little hand into his.

Oh God. He wasn't supposed to be charming the three-year-old! It was the elder Fuller he wanted to have looking at him that way. Instead, Marissa was focused on laying out the blanket she'd brought.

"Hi," Kaylee said again. "Hi." She rested her head against his hip.

"Hi," he said, forcing a smile.

Yes. He had definitely entered another dimension of time and space. Where Autry Jones was in a park with a single mother and her three-year-old, about to eat sticky peanut butter and jelly sandwiches, which, granted, *were* his favorite.

Make your escape. Any ole excuse will do. Bolt, man! Bolt.

But Autry's feet stayed right where they were, his gaze transfixed on Marissa's lovely eyes and a beauty mark near her mouth. Now he was staring at her lips. Wanting to reach out and—

"Mr. Autry, you're lucky," Kaylee said, snagging his attention as she sat down.

"Because I'm here with you guys?" he asked, tapping the adorable little girl on the nose as he sat at a reasonable distance. Did she have to be so stinking cute?

She tilted her head as though that was a dumb answer. "Because you get to eat dessert first if you want. You're a grown-up."

"Ah," Autry said, smiling at Marissa. "But I always eat my healthy sandwich first. Then dessert."

Kaylee shrugged, turning to look in the bags. Marissa pulled out a jar of peanut butter, strawberry jam and a loaf of bread, then some paper plates and plastic utensils.

"Allow me," he said, taking the knife and peanut butter.

She raised an eyebrow. "I'm sorry, Autry, but you really don't strike me as a man who eats a lot of PB and J."

"You've never seen me at midnight, hungry for a snack while going over fiscal projections."

Her cheeks grew pink. Hmm. That could mean only one thing. That she was imagining him at midnight, naked, eating peanut butter in his kitchen. Not that that was remotely sexy. Maybe she was just imagining him at midnight. Naked or not. She still wasn't giving him any signals either way. She didn't flirt. She didn't laugh at every little thing he said, funny or not. She didn't brush up against him to try to turn him on. He really had no idea if Marissa Fuller, mother of three, was interested in him in the slightest.

They ate. They had sandwiches. They had oranges. They had chocolate chip cookies. By the time Autry almost finished his sparkling water, Kaylee had fallen fast asleep on the blanket, using her little monkey backpack as a pillow.

"Three kids, huh?" he said. "That can't be easy."

Marissa took a sip of her water. "It's not. But loving them is. Plus we live with my parents. In the house I grew up in. So I have backup 24/7."

He noticed she kept her gaze on him, as if waiting to be judged.

"*You're* the lucky one," Autry said. "If you live with your parents, you must be close with them. And your kids and folks must be close. That's gold, Marissa."

She tilted her head. "I guess I've never really thought of it that way. But you're right, we are close. Maybe too close!" She smiled. "Not you and your family?"

He looked up at an airplane high in the sky, watching it jet over the clouds. "No. We were never a close family. The Joneses were about business. Everything is about Jones Holdings, Inc. Interestingly, not even that managed to bring us closer. But I was never close with my brothers growing up. And there are five of us."

"But you're here," she said. "Visiting Walker and Hudson."

"I'm trying," he said. "My father, the imperious Walker Jones the Second, feels like his namesake eldest son defected. Walker moved here. Opened a Jones Holdings office here. Is doing what he wants—here. And Hudson always marched to his own drum, which never involved the family business."

"And you?" she asked. For a moment he was captivated by how the sun lit up her dark hair.

"All about business. But I try very hard not to be a workaholic. I never want to be like my father, who put the company above everything—family, birthdays, special occasions. He missed everything and still believes business comes first."

"You just said you're all about business," Marissa pointed out.

"Because I don't have other commitments or responsibilities. For a reason. No wife. No kids. When I work around the clock or fly off to Dubai for a month, I'm not hurting anyone. In fact, I'm making someone happy—my father."

"But surely you want a family someday," she said, popping a green grape into her mouth.

He reached for his water and took a long sip. Did he? If he were really honest, he didn't know. He'd had his heart smashed, his trust broken, and all his tender feelings for that sweet baby he'd come to think of as his own had hardened like steel.

"So you're divorced?" he asked, glad to change the subject. He wanted to know everything about Marissa Fuller.

"Widowed," she said, taking a container of strawberries from the bag. "Two years ago in a car accident. My five-year-old, Kiera, has very little memory of her father. Kaylee here has none at all."

"And the third daughter?"

"Abby. She's nine."

Nine? Marissa couldn't be older than twenty-seven, maybe twenty-eight. She'd been a mother a long time, practically all her adult life.

He watched her bite her lip, seeming lost in thought. "Abby was seven when her dad died and remembers him very well. A few times a week, when Abby is saying her good-nights to her little sisters, I'll overhear her telling them about their daddy."

Marissa's life was very different from his. What she'd been through. What she did on a daily basis.

"She sounds like a great kid," he said.

Marissa nodded. "And one who had to grow up too fast. She mothers her little sisters all the time. Sometimes I even forget that life before their dad died wasn't quite like the paradise Abby paints for her sisters."

Her cheeks turned red, as though she hadn't meant to say that aloud. She held out the container of strawberries and he took one.

"Well, I might not be married," Autry said, "but I

have no doubt that marriage is hard and takes work. And you clearly got married very young."

"I got pregnant on prom night. Married and a mother at eighteen. Four years later, Kiera came along. And Kaylee was a surprise—a nice surprise, but maybe not the boy Mike ho—" She turned away. "I guess sometimes I start talking about all this and end up saying too much."

He reached out and moved a strand of hair from her face, the slightest touch against her cheek, and yet he felt it *everywhere.* "Best way to get to know someone is to listen to them talk when they're not guarded."

She smiled. "You're trying to get to know me?"

"Well, I only have three weeks in Rust Creek Falls, but yes. I want to know you, Marissa Fuller."

"Marissa Fuller, mother of three. With baggage. With live-in parents. With a really busy schedule."

"I'd like to steal up your free time," he said.

She laughed. "Do I *have* free time? If I ever have time to myself, I always think I should spend it one-on-one with one of the girls. Or I should scrub the bathroom tub before my mother does, and she always gets to it before I can. My life isn't exactly Italian restaurants and dancing and walks in big-sky country."

He moved a bit closer to her. "But maybe you'd *like* to go to dinner at an Italian restaurant. Go dancing. Take a walk in big-sky country."

"I'd love all that, Autry. But I've got responsibilities. Three young kids."

He nodded. "Of course. But do you know who you sound a little bit like? My dad. He never felt comfortable taking a day off. He never relaxed or had fun. The business was everything, just like your home life is. As it should be, Marissa. Home and family—that's everything. But you need some time to yourself, too. To recharge."

"I wish," she said. "But I've been doing this since I was eighteen, Autry. You're what? Thirty-two? Thirty-three? I can't even relate to that kind of freedom. I hear you jet all over the world for Jones Holdings."

"Thirty-three and, yes, I do. Our corporate headquarters are in Tulsa, Oklahoma, where I grew up. I live in a skyscraper on the twenty-fifth floor. But I'm never there. I have a whole atlas of destinations in mind to build our corporate profile and assets."

"And no woman has ever tempted you to settle down? Like your brothers?"

He frowned and turned away, hoping his expression didn't match what he was thinking. He didn't want to talk about Karinna or Lulu. "I don't have the luxury of that," he said. "Not if I want to keep Jones Holdings expanding globally. Just like you don't have the luxury of going to a movie whenever you feel like it. In three weeks, I'll be in Paris, likely for a year." He paused and looked directly at her. "Maybe until I leave, we can keep each other company."

"Exsqueeze me?"

He laughed. "I don't mean in bed. I mean I'd like to spend time with you."

"I'm a package deal, Autry. Even for three weeks in August."

"Kaylee likes me," he said. "I've already passed the Fuller daughter test."

Marissa smiled. "I suppose you have. She's not easy to charm." She took a long sip of water. "Look, Autry.

You're tempting. Very tempting. But my life isn't about fantasy or what I think about before I drift off to sleep."

"Doesn't mean you can't have a little romance in your life."

"Romance? I think I'm done with that, Autry."

"Marissa—"

She took a deep breath. "My marriage wasn't perfect. Many nights, Mike and I went to bed angry. It wasn't easy for me to juggle working full-time with having three little kids and trying to take care of a home, so I became a stay-at-home mom. Money was tight, and Mike worked longer hours at the office to secure a promotion and a raise. We argued at times, the stress made it impossible not to, but we both agreed the sacrifices were worth it. Thing was, with so many added responsibilities, romance went out the window. That's just the way it was and I wasn't about to complain. I knew I had a blessed life. A home, a good husband, three healthy children. Till that one day when a drunk driver took Mike away."

"I'm so sorry."

She nodded. "I was so overwhelmed by grief and panic. I wasn't really sure how I'd keep things going, but I just kept putting one foot in front of the other for the kids. The meager life insurance policy that Mike had helped for a while, but I worried about money constantly. So when my parents suggested we move in, I said yes. Ralph and Roberta Rafferty are wonderful grandparents, but I'm a twenty-seven-year-old woman living at home with Mom and Dad."

"I admire you, Marissa. You did what you had to do at every step."

He thought about how tough her life was—reward-

ing and full of love, yes, but tough. He didn't date
single mothers, but if he couldn't break his own rule,
what good was it? For the three weeks he had in Rust
Creek Falls he wanted to give her the world. Her and
her kids. It wasn't like he'd fall in love. Marissa was a
single mother of three. There was already a great bar-
rier built right in.

"Well, I'd like to get to know you while I'm here,"
he said. "I'd like to treat you and your daughters to a
little fun. Good clean fun like this picnic. Hot-air bal-
loon rides. Baseball games. You name it." He paused.
"But clearly, I'm very attracted to you, Marissa. I think
you're drop-dead gorgeous. I like spending time with
you. I like *you*. So romance is definitely on my mind.
I just want to put that out there."

He'd enjoy his time with Marissa, cement a bond
with his brothers, repair things with them and his dad,
then he'd jet off to Paris—no heartache for either of
them.

She stared at him with those brown eyes, and again he
could see her thinking. Assessing. Considering. "You're
not looking for commitment and I'm not, either," Marissa finally said. "So…friends. No strings attached."

"No strings," he repeated.

But their agreement left him a bit uneasy. It was one
thing to say no strings and another to really mean it.
And hurting Marissa—or her kids—was unacceptable.

Chapter Four

At dinner that night, when it was Kaylee's turn to share something special that had happened that day, a Fuller-Rafferty tradition going back generations, the three-year-old couldn't stop talking about the nice man who came on their picnic and did magic tricks.

Yes, Autry Jones did magic tricks. The man was full of surprises. Big ones and little ones. At the two-hour mark of the unexpectedly long picnic, Marissa had had to wake up Kaylee so Autry could meet his brothers and Marissa could go pick up Kiera and Abby from their playdates, but Kaylee had been a little grumpy and still tired. Autry had plucked a clementine from the bag and made it magically disappear and reappear atop Kaylee's head, which had brought forth belly laughs and "do it again, Mr. Autry."

"Who was it?" Abby asked, reaching for the bowl of mashed potatoes.

Marissa slid a glance at her mother, who was pretending great interest in passing the platter of roast chicken to her husband, but was really hanging on to every word. Marissa didn't often spend time with any men. Nice or otherwise.

"While we were shopping for our picnic in Crawford's," Marissa explained, "we ran into someone I met at the viewing party last night. So we invited him to join us. No big deal."

"Who was that, dear?" Roberta Rafferty asked, so nonchalantly that Marissa smiled.

"Autry Jones."

Fifty-five-year-old Ralph Rafferty paused with his fork in midair. "Autry Jones? Is he one of the millionaire Jones brothers?"

Marissa knew Autry was rich. Filthy rich. And he looked it. But somehow, the man she'd gotten to know a bit last night and today was a bunch of other things before millionaire. Kind. Thoughtful. Patient. A good listener. And so insanely handsome that just thinking about his face—and yes, that amazing body—gave her goose bumps. "Yup. He's in town for three weeks visiting his brothers."

"Wait," Abby said, her brown eyes the size of saucers. "Do you mean to tell me that the man I saw with Walker and Hudson at the Ace came on your picnic?"

Marissa bit her lip. It was one thing for her daughter to notice a cute man for her mother to "date," never having known her mother to date. It was another for that to become a reality.

Abby frowned and stared at her.

Uh-oh. This was new territory for Marissa. Though technically, she and Autry weren't dating. They were friends. Who might kiss, maybe. Probably. Marissa sure hoped so.

"I can't believe I missed the picnic!" Abby's expression turned all dreamy, and if Marissa wasn't mistaken, cartoon hearts were shooting out of her chest. "So you're dating him? That's so exciting!"

Marissa glanced at her mother, whose expression was its usual granddaughters-are-watching-and-listening neutrality. Roberta Rafferty would let Marissa know her opinion loud and clear later, when the girls were in bed.

"Abby, Autry Jones and I are not dating. We're... friends. New friends, at that."

"He does magic tricks," Kaylee said. "Grandma, Grandpa, Mr. Autry made a little orange appear on my head!"

Her parents laughed, and mentally, Marissa thanked Kaylee for breaking the tension.

"So everyone knows him but me?" five-year-old Kiera asked, pushing her long brown hair behind her ears. "No fair."

"Well, Mr. Autry did offer to come over tomorrow night and make a special dinner," Marissa told her middle daughter. "Steaks and potatoes on the grill. Who wants to help make dessert for after?"

"Me-e-e!" a chorus of three trilled.

Again Marissa felt her mother's eyes on her. She added potatoes to her plate, despite not having much appetite. "Tomorrow is your night to cook, Mom, so it'll be nice for you to have a night off." Marissa, her mom and her great cook of a dad took turns feeding the family of six every night. She tried to imagine Autry

Jones wearing an apron. Flipping steaks on the grill. Sitting down to a meal with her entire family.

"Oh, I'm very much looking forward to grilled steak and potatoes," Roberta said. "And meeting Autry Jones."

Roberta's chin was a bit high, her eyes a bit narrowed, her expression a bit...motherish. A millionaire Jones brother in town for three weeks and mysteriously making dinner for the whole family tomorrow night? Marissa could read her very smart mother like a good book.

There was only one reason why such a man would do such a thing. Because he was physically attracted to Marissa. If and when the notch on his belt was made, his grilling days for the Fuller-Raffertys would be over.

Her mother did have a cynical streak that she defended as "reality," and quite frankly, so did Marissa. She was no one's fool. She knew when a man was attracted to her, and Autry Jones clearly was. But unless she'd suddenly turned naive—and after all she'd been through in life, she doubted it—Autry Jones wasn't a user, wasn't a wham-bam-thank-you-ma'am kind of guy. Her gut said so, anyway, and any time Marissa stopped listening to her gut, she paid the price.

Yes, indeed she, too, was looking forward to Autry coming over tomorrow. Maybe a little too much.

The next afternoon, Autry sat in a leather club chair in the lobby bar of Maverick Manor. He wished there were a Maverick Manor in all the destinations he found himself in. Autry had always been a glass and marble guy, appreciating clean lines and craftsmanship. Who knew he'd love a log-cabin-style hotel, albeit one that was pure luxury, bringing in big-sky country with great architectural detail and all the amenities? Maverick Manor soothed something inside of him, something he hadn't even been aware of. Out the windows was a breathtaking view of the Montana wilderness, and across the room a massive stone fireplace that almost made him wish it were winter. He glanced up at the mural above the reception desk featuring residents of Rust Creek Falls. The focus on community and family appealed to Autry, which surprised him. But then again, the call of family unity was really why he was in town in the first place instead of scuba diving at an Australian reef or working on his tan on the French Riviera.

He kept his gaze on the mural, uncomfortable with the scene a foot away from him. His brothers and their wives sat across from him with three babies. Little Jared sat on Hudson's lap, Katie on Bella's and Henry cuddled up against Walker and his wife, Lindsay, clutching a little monkey he was chewing on. The triplets were Bella's brother's children, and the Joneses were on babysitting duty while Jamie and his wife had a quiet lunch for two at the Ace in the Hole. The only reason Autry was able to tell which baby was which was because their names were stitched across their T-shirts. And Katie had a sparkly purple barrette in her dark blond hair.

"Talk to Dad lately?" Autry asked both brothers, watching their expressions.

He could tell by Walker's slight sigh that it wasn't a topic he was comfortable discussing. Hudson barely seemed interested at all.

"We have a scheduled call every Monday at ten thirty to go over business," Walker said.

Autry knew that. Autry had the eleven-o'clock slot with the Jones Holdings chairman. But he was referring to personal stuff. Family. Interests. Life in general. "Ever talk about anything besides business?"

Walker practically snorted. "With Dad?"

"Mom's as interested as Walker the Second," Hudson said. "Bella called Mom to ask for an old family recipe for the cheesecake we had every Sunday growing up. Mom said, 'Really, dear. The cook made that. I could look up her number if you'd like.'"

Bella smiled. "I was trying so hard to find some common ground that I said, 'Sure, give me the cook's number.' But she left it on a voice mail and that was that. No family bonding."

Autry threw up his hands. "What's it going to take?" His parents had come to the weddings and had been cordial and made the rounds, but all Autry's attempts at getting his mother or father to reveal some kind of hidden depth of joy that two of their sons had found love and happiness had been a waste of time. His mother had gone as far as to say Bella and Lindsay "were lovely young women," while his father had merely looked around and asked, "Where's the rest of the town?"

"Dad's still upset that he can't control me," Walker said. "I was the dutiful CEO, but when I said I was settling here and opening a Jones Holdings office, he never got over it."

Hudson shook his head. "I've been used to that for years. He'll never accept that I 'turned my back' on the family business and roamed the country. But if Mom and Dad want to be stubborn and spend the ten minutes a day they actually speak to each other talking about how we let them down, that's their business. I wish they could be happy for us. I wish they could be *happy*."

"Well, you did kind of shock us," Autry said. "No one expected either of you to settle down, let alone in a small Montana town."

"Sorry," Bella said, kissing her baby niece on the head. "Love struck."

"Sure did," Hudson said, reaching over to squeeze his wife's hand.

"And love is wonderful," Lindsay said. "To think that when I met Walker, we were on opposing sides of a courtroom, battling over a case involving Just Us Kids. Now, we're happily married."

Walker inched closer to his wife and gave her a kiss on the cheek.

Bella smiled. "When Hudson became my boss at the day care, I thought we'd be on opposing sides, too—the manager wanting things one way and the big boss insisting on things his way. But here we are, united."

"And thanks to Bella, I have the cutest nephews and niece in the world," Hudson said.

That was not in dispute and for a moment, the five of them just gazed at the adorable triplets.

"To be honest, Autry," Walker said, "I'm surprised Dad let you come here. Hudson and I figured he'd be afraid to let you anywhere near the town that so horribly influenced two of his sons."

"I'm my own man," Autry said. And he was. His father actually had spoken up against Autry spending such a long time in Rust Creek Falls.

Just don't drink the water, dear, his mother had said. *Or the punch, actually. I overheard a group joking about how someone spiked the punch at a wedding in*

Rust Creek Falls with some kind of magic love potion. It's no wonder your brothers fell prey.

Fell prey. To love.

Don't you want your sons to be happy? Autry had asked her. *Because they are.*

Of course I do, she'd said. *But my goodness, Autry, there are surer paths.*

Autry had almost said "How on earth would you know?" but he'd held his tongue. He hadn't been about to start an argument at a charity fund-raiser.

"I'll toast to that," Hudson said, lifting the baby on his lap. "To being your own man, little guy," he said, then blew a raspberry on the one-year-old's tummy.

"And to being your own woman," Bella said, giving Katie a little lift above her lap. Baby Jared cooed. Everyone laughed, which broke the tension that had gripped the air.

"Oh—I see my friend Tom over by the bar," Hudson said, upping his chin at a tall man across the room. "Excuse me for a minute to go say hi. Take this little guy, Autry?" his brother asked, and without waiting for a response, handed him over.

Autry swallowed. He couldn't exactly thrust the baby back to him, not with his sisters-in-law and Walker watching. Even if that was exactly what he wanted to do.

Jared sat on his lap, looking up at Autry with giant eyes while holding out his little chew toy.

"Thanks for being willing to share, but I have all my permanent teeth," Autry said.

Lindsay laughed, pushing her long brown hair behind her shoulder. "I give you a C-plus in toddler talk, but an A-plus for trying."

Bella nodded. "Jared sure seems to like you."

Autry forced a smile at his sisters-in-law, then glanced down at the sweet-smelling baby. Lulu had sure seemed to like him, too. She was three months old when he fell in love with Karinna, and for the six months their relationship lasted, Autry had felt like a father. He hadn't thought he had it in him to be a dad until Lulu taught him that it came naturally. You loved. You showed up. You cared. You committed. You took responsibility. That baby girl had sneaked her way into his heart within hours. But she wasn't Autry's. She wasn't his daughter, didn't have his DNA, and Autry had had no claim on her when Karinna had broken up with him. He'd tried to see Lulu, asked if he could stay in her life, take her to the zoo once a week, anything, but Karinna had coldly reminded him he wasn't her father, and he'd never seen the little girl again.

That old bite of anger poked him in the heart and he shifted on the seat, his collar getting tight, his heart rate speeding up. Luckily, Hudson came back just then and scooped up his nephew, and Autry excused himself to go to the bar for a club soda he didn't want. He needed to get away, needed air.

But in just a few hours, he was due over at Marissa Fuller's house to make dinner for her, her three kids and her parents. His idea. He and Marissa had been about to part on Cedar Street, Autry going one way, Marissa the other, and he couldn't bear the thought of leaving her without having a plan set up to see her again. He couldn't ask her on a date with Kaylee's big ears listening. And he wasn't sure she'd agree to a date after their conversation. So in the middle of the intersection, he'd found himself suggesting he grill for the

Fuller-Raffertys—safe, family friendly, romance kill-ing. He'd also figured he could get a sense of what her life was like while living with her parents and raising three kids on her own, just how chaotic it was. Maybe by the time he'd flipped the steaks he'd be ready to run screaming for his hotel. He was kind of hoping that would be case, that something would obliterate his at-traction to Marissa.

But despite knowing she had three kids, he couldn't wait to see her, couldn't wait to meet her other two daughters. Which made no sense. He wasn't supposed to be so interested in her as a *person*, just as a sexy woman. A very enticing, sexy woman.

What the hell had he done?

And how was he going to get out of it?

Chapter Five

While Abby read a novel on her summer reading list and the two younger Fuller girls played "school" with stuffed animals in the family room, Marissa and her mother made a salad. Dessert, a chocolate cake that everyone had helped with, was cooling on the windowsill.

Marissa glanced at the clock on the wall. It was five forty-five. Autry was due at six. Her toes tingled. For real. And her heart was beating a bit too quickly. She couldn't stop picturing Autry's face, those gorgeous blue eyes, his strong jaw and sexy tousle of dark blond hair. And all that height, and the muscles, the deep voice with the Oklahoma drawl.

"Marissa, you're mauling the poor lettuce," her mother said beside her.

Marissa glanced down at the big wooden bowl. "Just a little preoccupied, I guess."

Roberta Rafferty glanced into the family room to make sure big ears weren't listening. Between the *Fro-*

zen soundtrack playing softly on a speaker and her mother whispering, it seemed safe. "*Is* this a date?"

"No." An honest answer. This was a new friend, temporarily in town, coming over for dinner. To make dinner. She said as much.

Her mom chopped tomatoes and added them to the bowl. "Well, a single man is coming over to a single woman's home to make dinner for her entire family. I'd say it's not only a date, but that you skipped a few steps. He's meeting your children *and* your parents."

"Because it's not a date. We're just friends. A date would imply the possibility of a future. Autry is leaving town at the end of August for Paris. I think he'll be there at least a year. This is only about friendship."

"I just don't want to see you get hurt," Roberta said, slicing a cucumber. "Three weeks is enough time to fall head over heels in love, Marissa. And get your heart broken."

"Mom, come on. When have you known me to be anything but pragmatic?" Okay, fine, she'd gotten pregnant on prom night. But by the man she'd always intended to spend her life with. She hadn't let Mike Fuller unzip her fancy pink satin prom dress on a whim or impulse.

"I'm just saying be careful, honey. Autry Jones is from another world and if he looks anything like his brothers, a very handsome other world. You could get very hurt. And so could the girls."

Marissa stopped adding croutons to the salad and faced her mother. "How would they get hurt?" she whispered.

"Look, I don't know Autry Jones. I haven't even met the man. But that he's coming here to cook dinner for us says he's kind and gallant and charming and who knows what else. A millionaire businessman who does magic tricks? Kaylee already adores him. He'll have Kiera talking about him nonstop next. And Abby? She's nine and already talking about you dating Autry. Then, just like that—" she snapped her fingers "—he'll be gone and completely out of their lives."

"I told Abby he's just a friend and that's the truth. We are not dating. I know he's leaving town in three weeks. I'm not stupid, Mom."

Marissa's cell phone rang. Autry. They'd programmed their numbers into their phones at the end of the picnic. Was he calling to cancel? She answered quickly, eager to escape this inquisition.

"Hi, Autry," she said, walking toward the other side of the kitchen for a little more privacy. Of course she felt her mother's eyes boring into her back.

"Hi," he said. And then he paused.

He was canceling. He must have realized how crazy it was to start a friendship—when they were both clearly very attracted to each other—given that he was leaving in three weeks. Well, one of them had to be wise about this, and if she was rationalizing, at least he wasn't.

"Autry, are you there?"

He cleared his throat. "I just thought I'd make sure you had briquettes or gas for your grill," he said. "I could pick them up otherwise."

Not canceling. Neither of them was being wise.

"We have all that," she said. "You really do think of everything."

"Not always." He didn't elaborate.

"Me, either," she said.

He laughed, warm, rich and real, and her heart pinged just enough to let her know she was stepping into trouble territory. Shared worry over their situation was one thing they had in common.

Ten minutes later, the doorbell rang, and her younger daughters leaped up excitedly and raced to the door. Abby hung back a little out of shyness, Marissa figured.

Her mother raised an eyebrow.

Okay, maybe she was being a little stupid about this, in terms of ignoring the very gentle warning bell that said she was being reckless. Because this might not be a date, but she thought of herself in Autry's arms, kissing him, his hands on her, and that meant she didn't think of him as only a friend. But she'd have to. And Marisa Fuller was the queen of "have to."

Well, he'd *tried* to cancel.

But when he'd heard Marissa's voice, all thought had gone out of his head. He'd stopped thinking about how scorched he'd felt holding Hudson's baby nephew. He'd stopped hearing his motto, Do Not Date Single Mothers. He'd stopped picturing himself sitting in Marissa's backyard, three kids surrounding him.

All he'd heard was Marissa's melodic voice. All he'd seen was her face, her dark eyes. And all he'd thought about was her story, everything she'd gone through, how strong she'd been. And he was going to cancel on making her dinner because he was a one-hundred-eighty-pound weakling? No. They'd shaken on friendship and he was going to be a friend to her. Friends didn't cancel because they ran scared. Friends came through. And Autry had promised a delicious steak dinner, grilled by him, and the Fuller-Rafferty clan was not going to be let down.

The door opened and three girls beamed at him.

"Hi, Mr. Autry!" Kaylee said, waving at him.

He smiled at the adorable little girl. "Hi, Kaylee." He turned to the five-year-old with wavy, shoulder-length brown hair. "And you must be Kiera. It's very nice to meet you." The two younger girls ran onto the porch, and he could see Marissa and her parents behind Abby, who stood in the doorway.

"Do you know who I am?" the nine-year-old asked.

"Hmm," Autry said, putting down one of the two large bags he was holding. "Are you the Fuller girl who likes a band called 2LOVEU?"

The girl's face lit up. "They're my favorite!"

"Then you'll probably like this," Autry said, handing her a small wrapped box.

"What's that?" Marissa asked, looking from the gift in Abby's hand to him.

"What is it, Abby?" Kiera asked, as both younger girls rushed over.

Abby opened it and gasped. It was a small snow globe with the 2LOVEU band members inside, "singing" into a shared microphone.

"And look," Autry said, turning the snow globe upside down in Abby's hand. "Twist that and see what happens."

Abby twisted the little metal prong. A 2LOVEU song began playing. "It's a musical snow globe! Oh, thank you, Mr. Autry!" she exclaimed, wrapping her arms around him.

"You're very welcome," he said. "Wait, what's this?"

he said, pulling something else from the bag. "This one has Kiera's name on it."

Kiera grinned. "For me?" She opened her present and hugged it to her. It was a remote control miniature robot puppy. Marissa had mentioned that Kiera was obsessed with puppies, and since getting one wasn't in the cards, a robotic version seemed a good choice. "I love him! I'm naming him Fluffers."

"I see one more gift in the bag," Autry said, kneeling down and pulling out the small wrapped box. "This one has your name on it, Kaylee."

Kaylee jumped up and clapped. She tore off the wrapping paper. "Yay! Mommy, look! It's a stuffed monkey! I love monkeys!"

Autry smiled. "And when you press its tummy, the stars on his belly glow in the dark." He remembered Marissa mentioning at the picnic that Kaylee often woke up in the middle of the night. Maybe the glowing monkey would help soothe her back to sleep. And her mom could get a better night's rest.

A chorus of thank-yous from the girls had him smiling. "You're welcome."

"You didn't have to get them gifts," Marissa said. "But that was very kind. Thank you."

"It was my pleasure," he said.

"Autry, this is my mother, Roberta Rafferty. Mom, Autry Jones."

The older woman standing beside Marissa did not look particularly happy, but she had a pleasant enough smile on her face. She looked a lot like Marissa. "Very nice to meet you."

"And this gentleman here is my father, Ralph Rafferty," Marissa said.

Her father shook Autry's hand and positively beamed. "It's an absolute pleasure to meet you, Autry. It's like meeting a celebrity. I read the business pages of the newspapers and often hear about the interesting deals and investments Jones Holdings, Inc. is involved in. I hear you're headed to Paris next—I read about the Thorpe Corporation negotiations."

"Hopefully all will go smoothly," Autry said. "It'll be one of our biggest deals." As he talked business with Ralph Rafferty for a bit, he couldn't help noticing that Marissa's mother seemed even more uneasy. "I'd better get this bag of groceries into the kitchen. Warm day today."

He picked up the brown bag and pulled out a bouquet of yellow tulips. "And just a little something for the lady of the house," he said, handing them to Marissa.

"Lovely," she said. "Thank you."

Marissa's father ushered the way into the kitchen, and Autry set down the bag. He could see the grill on the patio through the sliding glass door.

"I'll help Autry," Marissa said to her parents. "You two go relax."

"Dinner in one hour," Autry called. He pulled steaks, potatoes, asparagus, a small bottle of olive oil and a bulb of garlic from the bag. "All I need is the salt and pepper."

She brought over the salt and pepper shakers. "Do you always make this grand of an entrance?"

"I'll be very honest here, Marissa. I do when I want to. I have the means, and right now, I have the time. So I went shopping."

"But you couldn't have gotten those gifts in Rust

Creek Falls," she said. "We don't have a toy store. And Crawford's General Store doesn't sell those items you bought."

"Like I said, I have the time. Plus, driving to Kalispell gave me a chance to sightsee a little."

"And what do you think of the area?" she asked.

"It's beautiful," he said, seasoning the steaks. "Gorgeous open country. You can think out here. There aren't a million distractions. Just fresh air, nature, land, sky. I could have driven around for days."

She smiled then picked up the potatoes. "I like to brush the potato skins with olive oil before grilling them."

"Me, too," he said. While she put back the salt and pepper shakers, he stole a good long look at her. Tonight she wore a light blue tank top with ruffles along the neckline and a white denim skirt and flat silver sandals. Her hair was in a low ponytail, showing off her long, lovely neck. She was so beautiful and very likely had no idea. The only jewelry she wore was a silver watch on one wrist and a macramé bracelet that one of her daughters likely made on the other.

They headed out to the grill with the potatoes, to get those going, since they'd take the most time. Then they sat on the low stone wall separating the patio from the yard. He couldn't stop looking at Marissa's long, tanned legs.

The girls burst into the yard, Marissa's parents behind them. He pulled his attention from Marissa to the five people now crowding around them.

"Play it again, Abby!" Kiera said, twisting her little body into some kind of strange pose.

Abby turned the prong on the bottom of the snow

globe and the 2LOVEU song filled the backyard. She set it down and all three girls started dancing.

"I like how they dance without moving their feet," Autry whispered to the grown-ups.

Marissa laughed. "That's how it is now. It's all about the arms."

He was about to ask Marissa if she'd like to dance, but again he felt the weight of Roberta Rafferty's presence, her…disapproval, if that was the right word. Not of him, necessarily, but of them: him and Marissa. Millionaire Playboy Courting Single Mom of Three Who Lives with Her Folks. It did seem an unlikely headline. But he wasn't courting Marissa. He was going to be her friend—a friend of the family. And a good one. The Fuller-Raffertys had been through so much and if he could ease their burden and bring smiles, why not?

Except Marissa's mother wasn't smiling. She looked worried.

Because she probably thinks you're going to crush her daughter's heart and leave her kids asking what happened to Mommy's nice, generous boyfriend.

God, he was an idiot. Of course. He had to be careful here. He and Marissa had an understanding—a strings-free friendship—but her children were young and impressionable. He needed to take care with their feelings and expectations. No wonder Marissa had commented on the "grand entrance." He'd come to town with housewarming gifts for his brothers and sisters-in-law, a few toys each for Hudson's nephews and niece, and even some things for Just Us Kids. Five long, colorful beanbags that contorted into chairs and little beds, which had arrived yesterday. It was natural for Autry to come bearing gifts. He wasn't throwing his money around; he just enjoyed giving.

As the crew decided to play charades in the yard, Autry finally put the steaks on the grill. He couldn't help laughing at the kids' antics. And the way their grandparents accommodated their various ages, making each feel understood, smart and special, was something to behold. He could see Marissa's love for her daughters in her face, in her actions, in her words, and he hoped this family knew how lucky they were. They'd had their share of sorrow, but what they had here was priceless. And Autry knew it. Growing up, Autry's family life revolved around competition. Not love.

Fifteen minutes later, he announced it was chow time, and everyone sat around the big round table under the umbrella, digging into their steaks and baked potatoes and asparagus.

"Who wants to share first?" Marissa asked, looking around the table.

Autry raised his eyebrow and Marissa explained that it was family tradition at dinner for everyone to share something about their day—something that made them happy or sad, made them laugh or cry.

The Jones family had never done anything like that. In fact, they'd rarely eaten dinner together. His father had seldom been home, spending most of his time either at the office or traveling. His mother was on every board and charity imaginable. And his brothers had various team sports and clubs, so it wasn't often anyone was home at the same time. The family housekeeper and cook always had individual portions for any of them to heat up. But Autry had become a regular at his favorite pizzeria in Tulsa. The same-age teenager who worked behind the counter had become a close friend.

"Me!" Kaylee said, raising her hand. "I saw a butterfly. It was white. But I couldn't catch it. So I was happy and sad."

Roberta smiled. "I love butterflies. I'll share that I came home from having lunch with an old friend to find my dear husband reading *Jack and the Beanstalk* to his granddaughters, who were all curled around him on the couch. That made me very happy."

"Hey, that was my share," Ralph mock-complained.

"What about you, Mom?" Abby asked. "What's your share today?"

"I'll share that it's nice to make a new friend," Marissa said carefully, looking at her daughters. Then she smiled at Autry.

"I made a new friend, too," Kiera said. "A beagle named Maddy. When Grandpa took us to Crawford's today for ice cream after lunch, Maddy was outside. I asked if I could pet her and the lady said yes."

"I pet the dog, too," Kaylee said, beaming.

"Your turn, Autry," Abby said.

All eyes swung to Mr. Jones.

"I'll share that it's really, really, really nice to be here with all of you," he said. "You're a great family."

That even got a genuine smile out of Roberta Rafferty.

"Want to know my share?" Abby asked. "This," she said, taking her musical snow globe from her lap and placing it next to her plate. "I love this so much I could totally burst."

Autry smiled. "I'm glad."

With all the sharing done, the group dug in again,

eating, chatting, laughing. Why had Autry thought spending time with this family would be difficult? It wasn't. Kaylee, Kiera and Abby were fun to be around. They didn't remind him of what had happened with Lulu and Karinna, but then again, they weren't babies. And he wasn't romantically involved with Marissa. As long as he kept a reasonable emotional distance and didn't cross a line, he could enjoy Marissa's company and share in her life for the next few weeks. If he could bring a smile to the family, all the better.

But as plates were cleared and a delicious-looking chocolate cake was brought out, Autry realized he could stay here all night, quite happily. Despite being asked four times in the past twenty minutes by Kaylee why his shirt was blue. Despite having Kiera tell him a very long story about how beagles have three colors and how her grandpa helped her do research on beagles online after meeting Maddy. Despite listening to Abby talk about the lead singer of a boy band, a "totally dreamy Lyle," who had dimples and the greenest eyes ever and did Autry know that Lyle's favorite food was cheeseburgers and how, according to *Kidz Now* magazine, Lyle couldn't decide between ice cream or cupcakes as his favorite dessert.

It was a novelty, that was all, Autry realized. He'd avoided single mothers for a while now, so this kind of get-together was new and fun. Ah. Now that it made sense, Autry relaxed. Of course. He liked novelty. It was why he enjoyed his job so much. Flying to new and different destinations a couple times a month. Brushing up on foreign languages and learning about different cultures. He loved it. And the Fuller-Rafferty family was as different a culture as Autry could get.

"Well," Ralph said, looking at his granddaughters. "Since Mr. Autry was kind enough to make this amazing dinner, let's go into the kitchen and clean up."

There were groans of "Can't we stay out here with Mr. Autry?" But the girls dutifully followed their grandparents inside.

"Thanks for all this," Marissa said. "You made them feel special."

"Good," he said.

"And potentially not so good. Come September, you'll be long gone. But they'll still be here, living in this house, living the same lives. Maybe it's better that you don't set up too many expectations. So no more gifts, okay? You're Mommy's new friend and they're not used to my friends bringing over presents except for the occasional bagels and cream cheese on Sunday mornings."

"Understood," he said. "I'm not used to wanting to kiss my friends." And, man, did he want to kiss her.

She stared at him, biting her lip. Maybe he shouldn't have said that.

"Me, too," she said.

But kissing was out. Even if they'd sort of okayed it, okayed a "let's see" with no strings, no expectations. There were always expectations of some kind or another.

"Are those your initials?" he asked, gesturing at the big oak tree at the end of the yard.

She glanced at the tree, at the two sets of initials carved into a heart—MR+MF—and if Autry wasn't mistaken, a mix of sadness and relief crossed her pretty face. "We carved that with a key when I was sixteen." Sadness that Mike Fuller was gone, he guessed. Relief that the reminder of MR and MF took her away from this "whatever" with the man standing beside her. Him.

Autry headed over, touching the initials. "You have such an amazing sense of history and family here," he said.

She tilted her head at him, and he got the feeling she was surprised by his high regard for family, despite what he'd told her about his own. She took his hand and led him around the big tree, then pointed at a spot on the ground. "I tried to climb this tree when I was five, but fell out and broke my ankle. Twenty-some years later, Kiera made the attempt and sprained her foot. We're keeping it off-limits to Kaylee."

Marissa needed a hug, he thought. But the way she was looking at him, right into his eyes, he knew she wanted more than a hug. She wanted the man she was interested in to pull her close and kiss her, hold her tight. He could be wrong, but he'd bet his Tulsa condo on it.

He stepped closer, reaching a hand to her face, and tried to read what he saw in her expression. Desire. Conflict of interest. Exactly what had to be in his.

With the big old oak shielding them from view, he stepped even closer and kissed her—warm, soft, tingling. He could smell her shampoo. His lips opened slightly as she deepened the kiss, and it was all he could do not to lay her down on the grass and explore every inch of her.

At the sound of the sliding glass door opening, they each took a step back. "Until next time," he said.

"Should there be a next time?" Marissa asked.

"Probably not. But I hope there will be."

"Me, too," she whispered.

* * *

Later that night, after a long hot shower and a relaxing drink in his room, Autry called his father. He wished the Jones family could be different. That they could be close. That they could share what was going on in their lives—and not just whatever was related to business. Talk, vacation together, be…a family.

"Glad you called, Autry," Walker the Second said. "I was about to call you, actually. Convinced those two brothers of yours to move back home? Surely their wives would prefer a city like Tulsa over some backward small town. Not a high-end shop in the entire downtown. Your mother can't even imagine where they buy their clothes. Online, she figured. Did you know Rust Creek Falls doesn't even show up on a map of Montana?"

Well, the bad news was that his father was still focused on Autry convincing his brothers to move back to Tulsa. The good news? Walker the Second sure was chatty. That meant he was in a good mood and might be open to new ideas. Like that Autry's brothers were happy here.

"Dad, Walker and Hudson love it here. Lindsay and Bella love it here. They both have deep family ties in Rust Creek Falls."

"Well, Walker and Hudson have deep family ties in Tulsa. Where they belong."

"I don't think I've ever seen Walker so relaxed," Autry said, taking a sip of his Scotch.

"A relaxed Walker means a relaxed CEO," his father snapped. "And a relaxed CEO is the last thing any corporation needs."

"Jones Holdings is up this quarter," Autry reminded

his father. "He's doing something right. From Rust Creek Falls."

"Well, while you're there, talk up Tulsa with the wives. I'll even throw in a moving-home bonus—a world cruise for the four of them. Surely anyone could run the day care."

"They're very emotionally invested in Just Us Kids. The whole franchise," Autry said. Last night, Walker had told him how much it meant to him that kids had a safe, happy place to go while their parents worked, a place where loving, supportive caregivers and teachers met their needs. Autry had stared at him in astonishment, again amazed by the change in his eldest brother. *We were rich and had bored nannies who ignored us*, Walker had reminded him. *I want every kid who attends a Just Us Kids Day Care to feel happy and loved when they're in our care.* Autry tried explaining this to his dad.

He could just see his father, waving dismissively and groaning in his home library, where he liked to take family calls. "Look, Autry. A good business model has to account for what makes the company work. Cared-for kids is the point. I get it. But for God's sake, what the hell is Jones Holdings doing in the day care business? Rhetorical question at this point—I've had this conversation with Hudson and Walker for over a year and the answer never makes sense to me. Sure, it's profitable as a franchise. But it doesn't fit with our corporate profile. I dare say, it's almost a little embarrassing."

And Autry "dared say" that his father was a lost cause. But he wouldn't. Because he didn't believe it. Right now, the man was going through a shock to the system. Granted, it had been months since the "defection" of Walker and Hudson. He'd had plenty of time to adjust but still thought his sons would "come around."

They wouldn't. Autry had been in Rust Creek Falls a few days and could see that. This was home to Walker and Hudson. In every sense of the word.

"At least I don't have to worry about you, Autry," his dad said. "Can you imagine yourself falling for some local gal and settling down there?" His father snorted. "Ah, your mother is holding up her phone to show me the time—we have a benefit tonight. Look, Autry, I appreciate your trying to talk some sense into Walker and Hudson, but with you as president, traveling the globe, I know Jones Holdings won't lose its edge."

I have fallen for "some local gal," he wanted to say. But settling down here? That, he couldn't imagine. "Dad, it's pretty great here. I can see why Hudson and Walker moved to Rust Creek Falls. It's a special town and the people are friendly and welcoming. It's the kind of place that feels like home."

"Oh, good Lord," Walker the Second said. "You've got to be kidding me. Maybe I do have to worry about you now."

His father had nothing to worry about where Autry was concerned, but he didn't bother saying so. Walker Jones the Second wasn't really listening; he was talking. And what the person on the receiving end had to say didn't matter.

Autry wasn't sure he'd ever get through to his dad. As a strange sensation fluttered in his chest, he realized something had tightened, closed up, shuttered in his heart. All that family togetherness and sharing at the Fuller-Raffertys was nice, but it wasn't his life or his family. And he had to remember that. He wasn't here for love.

Stick to the plan, he told himself. *Show Marissa and her family a nice time while you're here. Make things easier for them.*

And the next time you feel the urge to kiss her behind an old tree with the whole history of her life in it, don't.

Chapter Six

Over the next few days, Autry was a regular visitor at the Fuller-Rafferty house. He made big country breakfasts of pancakes and bacon, grilled hot dogs and served his secret-recipe potato salad. He fixed two lopsided tables, sanded a door that stuck, talked the stock market with Marissa's dad and politics with her mother, listened to Abby go on about her favorite band and charmed the little Fuller girls with more magic tricks and stories about the exotic foods he'd tried in the different countries he'd traveled to. When all three girls wanted to try Indian food and spicy curry, he'd hired a personal chef to drive in from Kalispell and whip up a special feast.

"Must be nice to have so much disposable income," Roberta Rafferty had whispered with an edge of disapproval in her voice.

"Oh, for heaven's sake," Ralph had whispered back.

"The man is a millionaire. This is chump change to a Jones. I, for one, like Autry."

So did Marissa. So did her daughters.

Marissa had noted Autry was careful to limit their time together to family activities. They didn't go for solo walks. They didn't stand behind the big oak tree in the yard, where they could kiss in private.

They didn't have a second kiss.

But every night since their one and only kiss, Marissa had lain awake in her bed, staring at the ceiling, imagining herself under the covers with Autry. Sometimes she couldn't imagine it; she'd been with one man only, since she was sixteen. But then she let her fantasies take over and all thought poofed out of her head, instinct and desire running the show.

The other evening, when Autry had made them dinner and they'd gone around the table, sharing things, Marissa had really meant what she'd said—that she'd made a new friend. She'd let someone into her life. A friend, yes, but someone new. In the two years she'd been widowed, she hadn't done that. The first year, the single men of Rust Creek Falls had let her be, but by the second year, she'd found herself asked out quite a bit. In Crawford's General Store while picking up paper towels and milk. While waiting for Kiera and Kaylee at the day care both attended. Not that men were tripping over themselves to take her out, but at least twice a week she very politely declined invitations, and slowly, the asking had trickled down to a near stop. *She's not ready to date* was the echo Marissa sometimes overheard about herself if gossip came her way. And that was fine with her. She wasn't ready to date.

She knew she needed an Autry-free day so she could

collect herself, have a good talk with the practical, smart side of herself. If they were just friends—and that was what they were both trying so hard to be—she had to stop the nightly fantasies of him kissing her, making love to her, asking her to marry him.

It was that last one that had slapped her upside the head. What? Marry him? Where had the thought even come from? She couldn't possibly be subconsciously dreaming of marrying Autry Jones, could she? Maybe in some Cinderella-like fairy-tale sense. But Autry Jones was about global travel and would be gone in less than three weeks. And that would be that.

So today, with Grandma and Grandpa taking Kiera and Kaylee to a pottery painting class for three- to five-year-olds, Marissa was spending the morning with Abby, getting a trim for the nine-year-old at Bee's Beauty Parlor and then taking a trip to Daisy's Donut Shop. But as they were about to pass Crawford's General Store, Marissa noticed a crowd gathered in front of a table. There was an easel with a poster board on it, but too many tall men were blocking her view. Leah Ganley, president of the Rust Creek Falls K–8 PTO, sat behind the table with a clipboard.

"What's going on?" Marissa asked Haley Peterman, mother of a girl in Abby's class last year. Haley's daughter and two other girls were holding hands in a circle, talking excitedly about something. Marissa noticed Abby looking over at them shyly. Her daughter had her best friend, Janie, and a few other friends, but this clique of girls always seemed to have a sobering effect on her.

"The PTO came up with the idea to hold a kids' version of *The Great Roundup*," Haley said. "Isn't that precious? Young cowboys and cowgirls competing in Western challenges. The teams are going to be mothers and sons versus fathers and daughters. Ticket sales will benefit field trips for the coming school year."

When a group who'd just signed up moved away, Marissa could now see the poster. *The Great Roundup Kids Competition! Teams of mothers and sons vs fathers and daughters! Based on the TV show and for ages 8–12, The Great Roundup Kids Competition will feature our town's young cowboys and cowgirls and their folks in Western-style challenges on the town green, such as an obstacle course, ringtoss, three-legged race, piggyback rides and more!*

Marissa's stomach plummeted. Abby didn't have a father.

Haley Peterman seemed to remember that Marissa was a widow and turned around fast.

"Oh, look, it's Abby," one of the girls from her school said, and they inched closer. "Oh my God, it's so sad that you can't participate. Are you okay?"

"Why can't she?" another girl asked.

The ringleader turned and whispered something in her ear. Marissa thought she heard the word *dead*.

Abby's cheeks turned bright red and Marissa could see tears poking at her eyes.

"Aww, I think she's crying," a third girl said, before they turned and walked away.

"Sweetheart," Marissa said, kneeling down beside Abby.

But Abby's expression suddenly brightened and she raced off in the opposite direction.

Huh?

Marissa stood up and shielded her eyes from the

bright August morning sunshine to see who Abby had run to.

Autry Jones. Walking right toward her in sexy jeans and a brown Stetson.

"How are two of my favorite pe—" he started to say, before Abby flung herself against him, wrapping her arms around him.

Marissa headed over, watching Abby wipe away tears.

"Hey, what's wrong?" he asked, tilting up Abby's chin.

"There's going to be a kids' version of *The Great Roundup* and I really want to be in it. But it's mother-and-son teams and father-and-daughter teams. And I can't do it because—" Tears streamed down her cheeks.

"Abby," Marissa said. "I know it hurts. And I'm very sorry."

"But maybe Mr. Autry can be my partner," Abby said, wiping away her tears and looking up at him hopefully.

"Sweetheart, Mr. Autry has to prepare for his big business trip to Paris," Marissa said. "And The Great Roundup Kids Competition is an entire Saturday."

Marissa watched Autry glance over at the poster on the easel.

"I understand," Abby said, her expression crestfallen. "It's okay. Grandma always says we have to accept what we cannot change. Accept what I cannot change," she repeated. "Accept what I cannot change," she said again, as though trying to will the words from her head into her heart. And then she walked away and sat under a tree, her head down on her arms over her knees.

"If it's all right with you," Autry said, "I'll sign up with her."

"Oh, Autry," Marissa said. "You don't need to do that."

"Yes, I do. Because while her grandmother is right, you always have to have hope and believe in possibilities."

Marissa's eyes welled with tears. How was this man so kind? Why was he making it so impossible for her not to fall in love with him?

"If you really want to do it, it's more than okay with me," she said.

He smiled and squeezed her hand, then jogged over to Abby. Marissa watched as he told her daughter the good news and then Abby's face lit up. The girl jumped and flung herself at him and he wrapped her in a hug.

And Marissa caught his expression—uneasiness. A bit of sadness. She wondered what was behind it. Maybe he was just thinking that he was starting to like the Fullers and would be leaving soon, and would see Marissa and her daughters every now and then on trips to visit his brothers. Or maybe he really didn't want to do the kids competition but felt sorry for Abby and had spoken up before he thought too much.

Except from what he'd said, he didn't feel sorry for Abby. He wanted her always to know there were magical possibilities in life, even when it seemed there weren't. Yeah, her father was gone. But that didn't mean Autry Jones couldn't sign up in his place. And he had.

Marissa watched him head over with her daughter to the sign-up booth, saw the dropped jaws of Haley Peterman and the three mean girls from Abby's class.

"Mr. Autry is going to be my partner in the competition," she told the girls. "He rode his first horse when he was just three years old."

"Two, actually," Autry said, tipping his Stetson at Haley. Marissa watched the woman practically swoon.

"Actually, it's father-daughter," one girl said. "Right, Mrs. Ganley?" she said to the woman at the table.

"Well, that's just a label," Mrs. Ganley said. "But any adult can stand in for a parent or guardian. Aunt or uncle, family friend, that kind of thing. So Mr. Jones is welcome to sign up as Abby's teammate."

The girls' faces fell. Abby beamed. And Autry signed his name next to Abby's, making him her official partner for The Great Roundup Kids Competition in two weeks.

Autry took a flyer listing the challenges, like tug-of-war and an obstacle course, and handed one to Marissa. "We'll have to practice so we have a shot at winning the big prize." Free doughnuts for a month at Daisy's and a brand-new bicycle, compliments of the town mayor.

That meant Autry would be spending a lot of time at her house.

Uh-oh.

After a good ride on Hulk, one of his brother Hudson's mares, on the fields of the Lazy B ranch, Autry felt somewhat restored, a bit back to himself. He now stood under the shower spray in his suite at the Maverick Manor, the hot water coursing over him.

His mother was right. There had to be something in the goddamned punch. Not that he'd had any punch. But there was something in the water here in Rust Creek Falls, something that made previously normal people like himself turn inside out and sign up as the "dad" in a parent-kid competition.

Thing was, the minute he'd seen Abby Fuller's crumpled little face, the pain, the disappointment, the willing herself to accept what was, he'd remembered himself as a nine-year-old, a big house full of brothers he barely knew, his parents never around or interested in any of them as individuals. And he'd had both his parents alive and well. Abby had lost her father as a seven-year-old. If he could make things better, if just for a Saturday, hell yeah, he would.

He grabbed a thick, fluffy white towel and dried off, then wrapped it around his waist. Just as he stepped into his bedroom, there was a knock at the door.

He opened it, expecting to see Hudson or Walker. But Marissa Fuller stood there, cheeks pink, mouth slightly open.

"I…" she began, then turned away, and he remembered that he was just in a towel.

"Come on in," he said. "I'll go get dressed."

She stepped in and shut the door behind her, looking everywhere but at him. He smiled and held up a finger, then went into the bedroom and put on a navy T-shirt and jeans.

"I was just about to order room service," he said. "I'm craving a BLT and the Manor's peach iced tea. Join me?"

"That does sound good," she said.

He smiled and picked up the phone and placed the order.

"I can't even remember the last time I stayed in a hotel or ordered room service," she said, looking out the window at the gorgeous Montana wilderness.

"Actually, I can. It was my honeymoon when I was eighteen. We drove down to the Wyoming border and stayed at a motel in a tiny town even smaller than Rust Creek Falls. We just wanted to say we'd left the state." She smiled and turned to him. "It was just a plain room with dated furnishings and a lopsided bed, and there was no room service, but we were on top of the world for those three nights."

"I'll bet," he said. "You had each other and what else did you need?"

She tilted her head. "Exactly."

"Now here I come, wining and dining you with BLTs and peach iced tea and kid competitions involving a ringtoss and piggyback rides."

She laughed. "Well, when you put it that way, you don't sound like a millionaire jet-setter who's going to..." Her smile faded and she turned away.

He walked over to her and lifted her chin. "Who's going to what?"

"Leave."

He took a breath and nodded. "We always knew that, though, Marissa."

"Right. And we also shook on being friends. But..." She paused and dropped down on the love seat across from the fireplace.

"But things feel more than friendly between us," he finished for her. "There was that kiss, for one. And the fact that every time I see you I want to kiss you again."

"Ditto. See the problem?"

He smiled and sat down beside her. "Marissa, why did you come here? To tell me that doing the competition with Abby is a bad idea? That she's going to get too attached to me?"

"Yup."

"Except you didn't say that."

"Because I don't want to take it from her. I want her to be excited about the competition. To not lose out on something when she's been dealt a hard blow in life so young. But yeah, I am worried she's going to get too attached. All three girls. But especially Abby."

"Abby knows I'm leaving for Paris at the end of August. That's a given. Goodbye is already in the air, Marissa. We're not fooling anyone."

"Why do I keep fighting it, then?" she asked. "Why do I have to keep reminding myself that feeling the way I do about you is only going to—"

"Make you feel like crap when I go? I know. I've had that same talk with myself fifty times. I wasn't expecting to meet you, Marissa. Or want you so damned bad every time I see you."

It wasn't just about sex, but he wasn't putting that out there. If she kept it to sexual attraction, surface stuff, maybe he'd believe it. Then he could enjoy his time with Marissa and go in a couple weeks without much strain in his chest.

"So what do we do?" she asked. "Give in to this or be smart and stay nice and platonic?"

He reached for her hand. "I don't know."

"Your hair's still damp," she said. "I can smell your shampoo. And your soap."

He leaned closer and kissed her, his hands slipping around her shoulders, down her back, drawing her to him. He felt her stiffen for a second and then relax. "I don't want to just be friends, Marissa. I *want* you."

She kissed him back, her hands in his hair, and he could feel her breasts against his chest. He sucked in a breath, overwhelmed by desire, by need. "You're sure?" he asked, pulling back a bit to look at her, directly into her beautiful dark brown eyes.

"No, I'm not sure," she whispered. "I just know that I want you, too."

"Only when you're sure," he said, moving back a couple inches on the love seat. "You've got a lot going on, Marissa. I don't want this—" he wagged a hand between the two of them "—to mess up the order in your life. You have three girls to think about. You have a job. You have your parents."

"I know," she snapped. She took a deep breath. "Sorry. I guess sometimes I just wish I could have everything."

"Let me buy you a house," he said. "I could fund a bank account for you. You could quit your job."

She bolted up. *"What?"*

"To make things easier on you," he said.

"I have no interest in being anyone's kept woman," she said through gritted teeth, then marched to the door and left before he could try to explain that wasn't what he meant.

Dammit. He just wanted to make things easier. Really. Her own home. No need to work. After all she'd been through, why shouldn't she be able to relax a little?

Because she'd worked hard her whole life and had worked for everything she had. That's why. And she didn't grow up with the Jones millions.

He was about to run after her. Apologize. But maybe it was better that there was some friction between them. She wasn't sure about moving their "friendship" into the bedroom. And he knew it would only lead to problems when he'd have to say goodbye. So a little emotional space between them was probably a good thing.

So why did it make his chest ache?

Chapter Seven

Marissa hated when her mother turned out to be right, which was…always. "Mother knew best." Except when it came to Marissa the mother, who'd had a terrible lapse in judgment in allowing *that man* to sign up in The Great Roundup Kids Competition with her very impressionable nine-year-old daughter. A man who had zero scruples, obviously.

Buy her a house. Quit her job. He had to be kidding! That wasn't how life worked. You didn't make a wealthy man's acquaintance—one who'd be leaving very soon—and accept a free house and a padded bank account. And in exchange, he wouldn't have to feel bad about leaving Rust Creek Falls and the woman he'd dallied with. *But I bought the poor single mother a house and threw her some money!*

Marissa was so furious she could scream at the top of her lungs, but she was marching past Crawford's General Store, where groups were still signing up for the competition. What was she going to tell Abby? *Your knight in shining Gucci thinks he can buy me?*

By the time she got home, she'd worked out a plan. She'd tell Abby that something had come up and Autry Jones would not be able to do the competition with her. Some plan, she chided herself. Her daughter would be devastated. Tears poked her eyes.

"Marissa?" Roberta Rafferty asked as she came out of the kitchen.

Marissa stood by the front door, willing herself not to cry. "Where are the girls?"

"Your father took them to the park. Marissa, what's wrong?"

"Why would you think anything's wrong?" Marissa said. Then, with the kid-free okay to burst into tears, she couldn't stop herself.

Her mother pulled her against her and hugged her tight, then took her hand and led her into the living room—the "fancy" living room where no one ever went because the family room was the main hub of the house. Her mother sat her down on the brocade sofa and sat next to her. "Okay, tell me."

"It's nothing, Mom, really." Tears streamed. So much for nothing.

"Marissa, I know it's not easy living with me. You're a grown woman and a great mother and you have Mom overseeing everything you do and commenting. But I love you, honey. And you can always talk to me and expect me to give you advice that serves you—not me."

Marissa considered that. Her mother was fair. And she did often look the other way and bite her tongue when she didn't agree with how Marissa was handling something. The entire story poured out. How she and

Autry had shaken on being friends. How they'd kissed. How he'd signed up to be Abby's partner in The Great Roundup Kids Competition. How she'd gone to his hotel to tell him he could still get out of it, that Abby would understand he'd been pressured in the moment, and how they'd ended up kissing again and talking about how they had this mutual attraction. And then whammo, cold water on her head. He'd proposed buying her a house. Told her she could quit her job and he'd set her up for life.

"In exchange for?" her mother asked.

"Nothing," Marissa said. "He said he has the money, and after everything I've been through, he'd like to help and make all our lives more comfortable."

"Your dad would say to take that at face value."

"*You* wouldn't," Marissa pointed out.

"Maybe I would. I've been watching that man like a hawk the past week, Marissa. I've always prided myself on being a good judge of character. I don't think he meant anything…sordid by it. I think he meant exactly what he said. He does live in a different universe, Marissa. One where you jet off to foreign locales and spend money without a second thought. He grew up that way. But I'd judge him more on the fact that Abby was hurting and he stepped in—and up. That's a sign of who he is, Marissa."

Huh.

"And your reaction to his offer showed him who *you* are, honey," Roberta added. "I'm sure he's known women who would've jumped on it."

No doubt. And maybe, just maybe, Marissa was looking for anything to help her distance herself from Autry. But as her mom's words pushed past Marissa's defenses, she realized Roberta was right—as usual. Marissa wrapped her arms around her mother. "How did I get so lucky to have such a wise mother?"

Her mom squeezed her tight. "I will say this, though. I am worried that Abby is going to get very attached to Autry. She was already, and now, with practicing for the competition, she's going to worship him. She knows he'll be leaving, yes, but in her nine-year-old heart she may not understand that he'll still have to go—and isn't likely to be coming back. I do think you need to keep boundaries there."

Marissa nodded. The door opened and her father and the girls came in.

"Look who was walking up to the house when we got here!" Abby said. "Mr. Autry!"

Autry looked at Marissa, his gaze seeming to plead with her to give him a chance to explain. Little did he know her mother had done his work for him.

"Girls, I need to talk to Mr. Autry, so why don't you head into the family room for reading time?"

Abby ran over with a big smile. "Mr. Autry, after you and Mom talk, can we practice walking two hundred yards backward?"

Before Autry could respond, Roberta said, "Abby, you heard your mother. Right now it's reading time." Roberta then ushered the younger girls and a wide-eyed Abby into the family room. *Phew.*

Autry took a deep breath. "Marissa, I didn't mean—"

"I know. Now," she said. "My mother set me straight."

"You told your mother?" he asked, staring at her as though she had five heads.

"I guess we've gotten closer than I even realized.

I've been living here for two years. My mom has been my rock more than I ever knew."

"You're very lucky," he said. "No matter how hard it is sometimes to live with your parents, you're very, very lucky. I wish I were that close to my parents. I wish my father were my rock."

She nodded. "I forget sometimes." She squeezed his hand. "I shouldn't have thought you meant anything more than what you said. Everything you've done since you came into my life has been aboveboard and kind. I shouldn't have jumped to conclusions. But I've always worked for what I have, and providing for my family is my responsibility."

"You have no idea how much I admire you, Marissa Fuller."

She smiled. "Well, in that case, maybe you *can* spoil me a little bit. Take me out on the town tonight." She said it before she could think it through. But she would love a steak or seafood dinner in Kalispell, maybe some line dancing at the Ace, a drink in the fancy lobby of Maverick Manor. She would even put on her sandals with heels and a little perfume.

"You've got it. One night on the town coming up. But I need to ask. Right before our conversation went south, we were talking about the possibility of being more than friends. So is this a date or…"

This gorgeous, wonderful man was standing before her, wanting to give her a little highfalutin fun before he left in two weeks. Marissa knew he liked her, wanted her, but he'd be leaving regardless at the end of August. She could give in to the fantasy of being with him for these two weeks—with no strings. As long as she held on to reality, she'd be fine and maybe even better for it. He'd leave, but she'd have experienced something magical for a few weeks that would leave her in a good place mentally and emotionally.

Was she rationalizing an affair with Autry Jones, millionaire cowboy businessman? Maybe.

But so be it.

"I think we should let the evening decide where it goes," she said with a sexy smile she didn't even know she had in her.

The smile he returned went straight to her heart and her toes.

Just what would happen tonight?

Autry was getting ready for his date with Marissa when he heard a knock on his hotel room door. Marissa had wanted to meet him at the hotel instead of him picking her up, so that Abby, particularly, wouldn't see her mom clearly going out on a date with Autry.

But it wasn't Marissa standing in the doorway. It was Alexandra Lamoix, director of new business development at Jones Holdings, Inc. His father had hired her six months ago and she'd proved to be a valuable asset. She was a shark like his dad, which was useful in the boardroom. But she was so angelic looking that no one realized it until after her negotiations got her everything she wanted. Autry kind of admired her. And kept his distance.

"Alexandra?" He froze. If she was here, in person, something must have happened to his father. He felt the blood drain from his face and he grabbed the edge of the door to steady himself.

"I make you weak in the knees, I see," Alexandra purred in her raspy voice. She smiled, trailing a fin-

ger with a pale pink nail down the side of his cheek.
"I always knew it."

"What?" he said through the fog in his head. "Is
my father okay?"

"Your daddy's as fine as ever, darling."

His heartbeat returned to normal. "And you're here
because?"

"Well, I was passing through Montana on my way
to Seattle to research the Kenley Tech start-up, and
how could I not stop by and see you?"

Rust Creek Falls wasn't exactly a stop en route from
Tulsa to Seattle. She was here for a reason.

Alexandra stepped inside the room and glanced
around. Her long auburn hair fell, sleek and straight,
past her shoulders, and the very formfitting sleeveless
dress she wore with four-inch heels accentuated every
curve, including unusually large breasts. Delicate gold
jewelry decorated her neck and wrists. Yeah, he'd noticed her in the office back in Tulsa. It was impossible
not to, especially because she always stood very close
to him. That she wanted the chairman's son and CEO's
brother, the president of Jones Holdings, wasn't lost on
him. But tempted as he was once, Autry's trust meter
no longer let him down. *No, thanks, Alexandra.* She
might be attracted to him, but he'd be a stepping-stone
to her. And as enticing as she was on the outside, he
had zero attraction to what was inside.

"Sweetie, your daddy is worried about you," she
said. "We all are, on the executive floor of Jones Holdings. First we lost Walker the Third. Now you're here
in this two-bit town for weeks? Walker the Second is
worried you won't come back. So am I." She slid her
arms around him, her incredible breasts pressed against

him. "You know I've always had a soft spot for you, Autry. And I've come all this way to make my claim."

Unbelievable. He knew exactly what this was about. "My father sent you?"

"It was both our idea," she said, trailing a finger down his neck and pressing herself more firmly against him. "Come home where you belong. I'll take off the next two weeks and show you what a vacation *really* is, Autry Jones." She lifted her chin and puckered up her glossy red lips.

He heard a gasp.

It hadn't come from Alexandra. Or himself.

Autry looked behind Alexandra. Marissa stood in the doorway of his hotel room, shock on her face. She seemed frozen in place for a moment, then ran.

"Aww, is that a sweet lil local you picked up here?" Alexandra said. "What a quaint sundress."

"Go home, Alexandra. Now," he growled, and raced out. At the reception desk he quickly told the desk attendant to have the woman in his room escorted out and the door locked, then he rushed out of the hotel.

He looked in every direction. There she was. Marissa was running—slowly, in her heels—up the sidewalk. He caught up to her fast.

"Total honesty," he said, taking her arm. He'd just earned her trust back—thanks to help from her mother. There was no way in hell he was letting his father and his minions undo all that.

She wrenched it away from him.

He held up his hands. "Hear me out. Please. I may be a lot of things, Marissa, but I'm not a liar. Or a cheat."

She let out a breath, but at least she remained still and didn't bolt. Her hands were on her hips and she looked like she might snap a branch off a tree and conk him over the head with it.

"I was in my room—alone—getting ready for our date. Which I've been looking forward to more than anything for a very long time. Someone knocked and I thought it was you, but it was the director of new business development at Jones Holdings. Alexandra Lamoix. Turns out my father sent her to entice me out of Rust Creek Falls."

"Why?" she asked, dropping her hands to her sides. That was a good sign.

"Because he lost my brothers to this town. Or at least that's how Walker Jones the Second sees it. My brother Hudson always did his own thing, but Walker the Third was a company man, just like my father. Walker came here to handle the lawsuit against the day care and presto-chango, he now lives here. Built a Jones Holdings office building here. First Hudson settled down in Rust Creek Falls, then Walker. Now I'm visiting and my father is worried whatever's in the water will get me, too."

Marissa smiled. "Well, maybe he *should* be. Town legend says that because Homer Gilmore spiked the punch at Jennifer and Braden Traub's wedding, inhibitions were loosened and that started a love and baby bonanza. Some say the magic love potion has been in the air ever since."

"Well, there's no way that would affect me," he said. "I'm immune."

She raised an eyebrow. "Immune to love?"

"To babies," he said, turning away. "Family life isn't for me."

"To babies? But how? Why? You're great with kids. My kids adore you."

"Well, it's easy to be nice to everyone when I know there are no strings," he said. "I'm leaving in two weeks."

"And if you lived here?" she asked, narrowing her eyes. "You never would have come up to my table at the Ace in the Hole with those beers?"

"I would have because I didn't know you were a single mother."

He could see a flash of hurt cross her expression. "And if you'd known?"

"I wouldn't have approached you."

She stepped back as though he'd struck her. "Well. Like you said, you're not a liar. And now that this is all out in the open, there's no reason for you to continue your…our…ridiculous acquaintanceship." She stomped off in her heels, then bent over, took off both sandals and marched away barefoot.

"Marissa, please wait," he said.

She turned around. "For what? So we can be 'friends'? We tried that. It didn't work. We tried setting up a date. It's turned into a disaster before it could even happen."

"You always knew that I'm going to leave town. Tonight, the rest of the time I'm here, why can't we just enjoy each other's company? We know what we know."

"Because I don't want to get hurt. Because I'm not a dummy. Because I won't let my kids get hurt by your grand gestures when they'll never see Mr. Autry again after August."

"I don't want to get hurt, either, Marissa. It's why I—" He turned away.

"Why you what?" she asked.

He shook his head. He didn't want to tell her about Karinna and Lulu. Why dredge up all that pain when he'd buried it deep? Talking about it would make him feel like a fool, the supposed business whisperer who couldn't see a hostile throw-over coming when it had been in bed with him the night before.

"Autry! Marissa!"

Autry turned to see Hudson wheeling his triplet nephews and niece in their choo-choo train of a stroller. He held up a hand.

"Jamie and Fallon are on a date night, so Bella and I are babysitting. Bella's making some complicated recipe for dinner, so I thought I'd take these three little climbers over to Daisy's to play in the toddler playhouse while I had a double shot of espresso."

Marissa smiled. "They are so precious. I know you're Katie," she said to the adorable little girl. "And one is Henry and the other Jared."

"Jared is in the middle," Hudson said. "The one chewing on his favorite teething monkey toy."

"You don't freak out handling all three yourself?" Autry asked.

"I'm an expert at babysitting triplet one-year-olds now. The trick is to keep them all in your field of vision. Not easy, but that's how you keep everyone safe and alive."

Marissa laughed. "Well, if you could use some hands, we're available."

"We are?" Autry asked. Maybe there was some kind of baby magic thing happening in this town if just the sight of these three cuties had worked on Marissa's mood. Not only was she not running off, she had volunteered them both to help out. That was a good sign.

Oh, wait. No, it wasn't. She'd volunteered them to help because of what he'd said about being immune to babies. She wanted to prove to him that he wasn't.

Because she didn't know why he drew the line at single mothers—or had until he'd met her. Because she didn't know what the sight of a baby did to his head and heart, reminding him of a loss that had scorched every bit of tenderness inside him.

"I would love some extra hands," Hudson said. "Thanks, Marissa." He turned to Autry. "Guess you're on baby duty, brother."

He'd get through the half hour or however long this would be. Because it was saving his relationship with Marissa. Saving their date.

Huh. His date had been saved by teething babies. But that still didn't mean he was changing his antibaby stance. The adorable small creatures got inside your heart—and could break it.

Chapter Eight

As they entered Daisy's Donut Shop, Hudson saw a good friend and asked if Marissa and Autry would watch the triplets while he took a breather with his buddy. Marissa was thrilled to say yes. It wasn't that long ago that her own brood were babies, but Marissa would always cherish the feeling of holding a baby against her, breathing in that delicious baby-shampoo scent and remembering another time in her life.

The first time she'd held a baby to her chest, she'd been just a teenager, and she'd been so scared that she would mess up, not know what to do. She'd picked up half of "how to be a mother" from a book on parenting and "your baby's first year," and the other half came from instinct. And from her own mother's help, even though sometimes she'd wanted to tell Roberta to stop hovering.

So while she took one triplet out of the stroller—Jared's little hands were raised, showing he wanted to be picked up—she felt all the warm, happy feelings in the region of her heart.

Autry approached the stroller for baby number two, looking slightly sick. The supposed immune-to-babies thing. Right. She'd give him ten seconds to fall under the "baby spell." Henry held out his arms, and Autry flicked open the five-point harness like a pro to lift him out. But he simply picked him up and set him down over the railing of the toddler play area. No cuddle, no kiss on the cheek, no baby talk.

He wasn't smiling. He wasn't watching the little guys. He was staring out the window at…nothing, as far as Marissa could see.

Huh. Maybe he truly wasn't interested in babies. Marissa took Katie out of her seat and couldn't resist holding her close and giving her silky blond hair a little caress.

"You're so precious," she cooed to the little girl. "You and your brothers. What a gift."

Autry looked at her then turned away completely, his hands jammed in his pockets.

She frowned, surprised that the triplets hadn't worked their magic on him. No spiked punch was necessary for a baby to have even the most reserved grown-up fawning and fussing and cooing; that was a baby's superpower. They were simply irresistible.

But Autry Jones did seem oddly immune.

She'd figured this would be a great opportunity for him to see how special babies and toddlers were, that they had a way of getting inside your heart and making you remember, making you dream, making you think about the future and possibilities. Babies were the future and they were the now.

The triplets crawled around in the toddler zone, kicking brightly colored plastic balls and crawling through little tunnels.

"I can't do this," Autry whispered. "I can't. I'm sorry." He turned away and headed across the shop, away from the tables.

Can't do what? Marissa wondered. What was going on?

Hudson came back and thanked her for watching the triplets, then told her to take a break and get herself a drink and a treat on him.

She headed over to where Autry stood. He stared down at the floor, not acknowledging her.

"What's wrong?" she whispered.

He turned to face her, then took her hand and led her over to the window. "The reason I'm no strings… The reason I don't date single mothers… The reason I'm never going to be a family man—" He stopped talking and ran a hand through his hair. "Last year I met a woman in New York City while on business. Karinna had a three-month-old baby. I fell for both of them pretty hard. I loved Lulu like she was my own child. She felt like mine."

Marissa's heart clenched, sensing from his tone that his story did not a have a happy ending.

"I went to a baby store and had a room in my condo decorated as a nursery," he continued. "Crib, mobile, swing, rocking chair. I had a stroller, a bookcase full of board books with edges Lulu could chew. A changing table stocked with diapers and baby ointment. And I, Autry Jones, changed more than a few diapers on that table."

Marissa smiled. She could imagine it, actually. From

the way he was with her kids, from the way he was with her.

"That baby girl, everything I felt, made me realize how wrong my parents had it. I was going to propose to Karinna, settle down and put family above business. I'd still do my job and do it well, but family would come first. But the night before I planned to ask Karinna to marry me, she told me she'd met someone else, a CEO of a famous corporation in New York and, sorry, but it was over."

"Oh, Autry, I'm so sorry."

"You want to know something? I realized pretty quickly that I was more upset about losing Lulu than I was about losing her mother. I tried to arrange some kind of visitation with Lulu, but Karinna reminded me that I wasn't Lulu's father and hung up. I never saw Lulu again. And it hurt like hell, Marissa."

She reached out a hand to him, and he looked so... conflicted that she wanted to wrap him in her arms and never let go.

"I've dated only single women since. No single mothers allowed within five feet."

"I'm closer than that right now," she said, offering a bit of a smile.

"I know. And sometimes, it's like all the blood in my veins has just stopped flowing."

"You feel this way and yet...you still accepted Kaylee's offer to come on that picnic the day after we met. You offered to be Abby's partner in The Great Roundup Kids Competition. There's a part of you that doesn't want to let go of what you once felt, Autry."

"Maybe. I tried to stay away from you, Marissa. I

can't. And your kids have made it even harder because they're so great."

She smiled. "Well, I think I understand you a little bit better now, Autry Jones."

"Let's go help my brother out," Autry said. "Now that I actually said all that out loud, those babies don't look so intimidating at the moment."

"You can always talk to me, Autry."

"I'm beginning to realize that. And that goes for you, too."

She squeezed his hand and held his gaze, and again she wanted to fling herself into his arms. But they were in the middle of Daisy's Donuts.

They walked over to the toddler zone and watched the triplets play. Marissa stepped over the railing and sat down to play catch—or almost catch—with little Jared, while Henry toddled around the busy wheel and Hudson played peekaboo with Katie. Autry stayed just outside the play zone, but facing it and watching them. A good sign. She noticed his expression was less tight. Not that it was relaxed—not by a long shot.

"Where's Uncle Hudson?" Hudson cooed at Katie, covering his face with his hands. "Here he is!" he said, opening his hands to show his face.

Katie giggled and threw a little plastic ball at him. Hudson erupted in laughter.

"You've really changed, bro," Autry said, a wistful look on his handsome face. "Rust Creek Falls agrees with you."

Hudson smiled and scooped up a runaway nephew, blowing a raspberry on his chest and then setting him back down to chase his brother. "I'm not sure I changed so much as this town brought out parts of me I didn't know existed."

"I know what you mean," Autry said and glanced at Marissa.

"Ooh, it's that way, is it?" Hudson said, wiggling his eyebrows.

Two spots of red appeared on Autry's cheeks and Marissa tried her best not to burst into laughter. "I'm going to get myself a latte. Autry, what can I get you?"

"Aren't I supposed to be taking *you* out on the town?"

She smiled. "I think I can handle one three-dollar beverage."

"I like the real thing, just coffee, black—a dark roast. And thank you."

When Marissa headed over to the counter, she heard Hudson say to Autry, "Told you this place would get to you."

She wanted to let them know she could hear them loud and clear, just in case they thought she couldn't. But then again, she was standing only ten feet away.

"It hasn't got me," Autry said. "I'm leaving in two weeks. I'm still glad I met the very beautiful Marissa, though. But Paris awaits. I'll be there at least a year. And then another destination, then another."

Autry glanced at her then, as if he wanted to under-score that. As if she didn't *know*. Really, it was as if he walked around with it in capital letters on his shirts: LEAVING AT THE END OF AUGUST.

Hudson eyed Marissa with a raised eyebrow. In his expression she read: *Yeah, we'll see, brother.*

"Dad's worried, though. He sent Alexandra from the

Tulsa office to lure me home. In fact, the timing was so bad it almost ruined things between me and Marissa."

"Or maybe the timing was good," Marissa said as she walked over with their coffees. "Because I did see that little display, we ended up here. And you ended up opening up to me."

"Well, that is definitely good," Hudson said. "But dear old Dad needs to mind his own business. Unfortunately, that's exactly what he thinks he's doing."

"Part of the reason I came to Rust Creek Falls was to try to smooth things over between Dad and you two. Not only haven't I achieved that, but now I've made things worse between Dad and me."

"You mean *Dad's* made things worse," Hudson said.

Autry glanced at his brother and seemed to consider that. He nodded.

"We all have to live our own lives," Hudson added. "What feels right to us. We can't live the life someone else maps out for us. Even when it's our own stubbornness that maps it out."

"Meaning?" Autry said.

Hudson scooped up two of the triplets and set them in the stroller, then went back for the third. "The meaning is different for everyone. Just think about it."

From Autry's expression, Marissa wasn't sure Autry wanted to think about that one.

"Well, time to get these tykes home for dinner. Thanks for lending a hand."

"Anytime," Marissa said. "I've become a master at keeping an eye on three kids."

Hudson grinned. "See you. Oh—and Bella and I would love to have you both over for dinner at the Lazy B sometime soon."

As though they were a couple, Marissa thought, her heart squeezing.

Autry clapped his brother on the back and held the door open for the enormous stroller, and they both watched Hudson navigate the stroller up the sidewalk. The guy could barely get two inches before he was descended on by a passerby stopping to peer in at the triplets.

"Uncle of the year," Autry said, shaking his head with a smile. "The guy who'd been the lonest of the lone wolves."

"So maybe change is possible," Marissa said, before she could stop herself. "Or like Hudson said, people and places bring out sides of you that you just never knew existed."

"Or you know they exist and you try to forget," Autry said.

She glanced at him, and his expression was a bit too neutral. Trying to forget hadn't worked with Autry; that was clear. But what was that Hudson had said about stubbornness? Autry's battle was with himself. Not babies. Not love. Not her.

They finished their coffees, and then she wrapped her arm around Autry's. "Let's go have that date," Marissa said. "It might be the only one. Who knows. But you agreed to take me out on the town tonight and I want it."

He took her hand, and this time his expression told her he was glad for the change in subject. "At your service."

As she and her gorgeous date walked up North Broomtail Road, Marissa imagined herself sitting in any number of restaurants, whether here in Rust Creek Falls or over in Kalispell, and she suddenly just wanted Autry Jones all to herself. She wanted to be alone with him. To talk to him about anything that might come up, and if they were having dinner somewhere in town, who knew who might be inadvertently eavesdropping?

Yes, Marissa was going to say it. *Do it now before you lose your nerve*, she told herself.

"Autry, I just remembered that Maverick Manor has room service."

He glanced at her, waiting.

"I'd like to have dinner there. On the balcony facing the wilderness."

He grinned, his beautiful blue eyes sparkling. "A private dinner for two. Nothing I'd like more."

"Unless that woman is still there, waiting for you," Marissa said. She really hoped not. A flash of Autry's coworker came to mind. All sleek and sophisticated in her four-inch heels. She wondered if that was Autry's type. Probably. But then again, when they'd met, Marissa was in a T-shirt and shorts and flip-flops, so maybe *she* was his type, too.

"I instructed the manager to escort her out and lock up behind her. If there was any issue, Nate Crawford himself would have called me. No worries."

"Your father won't be happy," she said.

"My father is never happy. Unless he's making money."

"Do you think you'll be able to smooth things over between him and your brothers?"

"I'd hoped so, but now I'm not so sure. My father doesn't seem to care about their happiness or what they want. Only what he wants for them and for himself. I can't imagine being a parent and feeling that way."

"Me, either. All I want is for my daughters to be happy. It's my job to raise them to be good, responsible adults—not to dictate their paths or futures."

He squeezed her hand. "Those three girls are very lucky to have you for a mother, Marissa."

She smiled and squeezed back, and then there it was—Maverick Manor, the luxurious log-cabin-style hotel looked so welcoming. She'd never had cause to be in here before today.

"Hope tongues don't wag," she said as they passed the reception desk. "Marisa Fuller seen entering Autry Jones's hotel room will spread like wildfire in this small town."

"I'll make it clear to the right big mouths that we're discussing business."

She laughed. "You know three people in this town. Your brothers and me."

"Au contraire. I've been here a week and have met a lot of folks. I spent an hour at the Ace in the Hole watching a reality TV show. I met the entire town."

"Oh yeah," she said. "I guess you did." Plus he was warm and friendly and talked to people everywhere he went.

He slid his key card into the lock on his door. Earlier, when she'd arrived to find that very sexy, well-dressed woman with her arms snaked around Autry's neck, her lips puckered for a kiss that, thankfully, Marissa had interrupted, she hadn't gotten a chance to look around. The room was masculine, clearly meant for a man on his own. Leather and wood and marble. The windows were huge and faced the gorgeous Montana wilderness in the distance.

"The room service menu is on the desk. Take a look. Anything you want will be yours tonight, Marissa."

"Filet mignon," she said, perusing the menu, grateful there were no prices. Everything was a fortune, no doubt. "I had that once at a wedding. Melted in my mouth."

He smiled. "Filet mignon for two and a bottle of red wine sounds good to me."

"Me, too."

He picked up the phone, made friendly small talk with Mariel, the front desk clerk, and then ordered, adding, "Mariel, Ms. Fuller and I are having a business meeting and shouldn't be disturbed beyond room service. Thanks." He hung up and smiled. "Done. Mariel is a bit of a chatterbox. The staff is instructed in discretion, but if she hears anyone gossiping about seeing you come in with me, she won't be able to resist telling them what she knows. 'Oh, it's nothing—they were just having a business meeting.'"

She grinned. "What business are we discussing?"

"Us," he said. "Our business." He stood very close to her and tilted up her chin. And then he kissed her.

"No discussion there," she said with a smile.

"Sometimes, Marissa, I operate best by not talking too much."

She kissed him back, wrapping her arms around his broad shoulders. And then he picked her up and carried her into the bedroom. In the dimmest recesses of her mind, she knew that room service would knock soon and that they could go only so far here. Safety net in place, she let him lay her down on his bed, let him cover her with his body, his hands in her hair, his mouth fused with hers. He pulled up a bit and slid his hands under the straps of her sundress, then lower to her lacy bra and the flesh underneath, which elicited a groan from him.

She felt the hard planes of his chest, the muscles of his arms, of his neck. She put her hands on either side of his face and looked into his eyes, his gorgeous, intelligent blue eyes. And she saw everything there she needed to know. That he didn't want to hurt her, but he would.

Marissa had been through loss that had knocked her to her knees, thrown her world into a tailspin. Sent her girls howling in grief.

Granted, Autry Jones would just be leaving town. Not dying. *A little perspective, Marissa.* But he'd break her heart nonetheless.

The question was would it be worth it? To experience him for these weeks. To make love. To *feel* love. Would it be worth it even though losing him would hurt like hell?

"Autry, do you agree with that old saying that it's better to have loved and lost than never to have loved at all?"

He leaned back a bit and trailed a finger along her neck. "I might have thought so. Before."

"Well, I think the answer has to be yes. That it's better. If I hadn't loved Mike, I wouldn't have those three precious girls. We lost him. But we had him. And we have some wonderful memories."

He nodded and sat up. Guess she'd killed the mood. But it was for the best. And she knew he knew it.

"I would rather not have known Karinna or Lulu,"

he said. "But I'm the only one who got hurt. And the memories I have twist my stomach in knots. Not so much anymore. Now there's just a void, but if I think about it, I feel bitter. And sometimes an old ache."

She turned all that over in her mind. His situation was very different from hers. But his experience with loving that little baby had taught him that he *could* love, that he could be a father figure, that he did believe that family should come first.

She started to tell him that, but a knock at the door let them know it was dinnertime.

A waiter wheeled in the cart and set everything up on the table on the balcony. Then they were alone again.

He gestured to the balcony. "So maybe we *should* discuss the business of us. How this is going to work so we do the least harm."

"I think we should go back to friendship, Autry. No kissing. No carrying anyone to a bed."

"I'll miss that," he said. "Especially that."

She smiled. "Are you okay with being Abby's partner in the competition?"

He nodded. "I won't break a promise, especially not to a kid. I told her I'd be her partner and I will be. I think tomorrow night we should all watch the second episode together, and then Abby and I can make a practice schedule. Sound good?"

"Sounds good."

But while she ate the melt-in-your-mouth filet mignon and sipped her wine, all she could think about was the man sitting across from her and what it had felt like to be in bed with him, even for all of five minutes. If she could enjoy his company, clothed and naked,

without falling in love, she'd give herself this glori-
ous fling before settling back down to everyday life.
But how could she not fall in love with Autry Jones?

Chapter Nine

In the Fuller-Rafferty kitchen the next night, Autry was making his specialty: homemade pigs in a blanket. His three helpers were next to him, Kaylee and Kiera on step stools. Kaylee was rolling the dough to smithereens, but Autry believed that pigs in a blanket were un-mess-up-able. They were just too delicious. Kiera cut a wedge of dough for each mini hot dog, and Abby rolled them.

"How are the chefs?" Marissa asked, coming into the kitchen.

"A-plus for everyone," Autry said. "These are about to go in the oven."

"I can't wait to eat them!" Kaylee said.

"Me, too," Kiera said.

Abby licked her lips. "Me, three!"

As Autry moved to the oven with the tray, he heard Abby whisper to her sisters, "This is what it's like to have a dad."

Kaylee tilted her head and stared at him.

Kiera ran over and hugged his leg.

Marissa had lost her smile, her complexion going white.

His heart lurched.

"I remember," Abby whispered to her sisters. "And it's just like this."

"It's nice," Kiera said.

Kaylee nodded.

Marissa forced a smile and backed out of the kitchen, presumably to give her daughters privacy, to have this moment for themselves.

As uncomfortable as the whole thing had made him, he learned right then everything he needed to know about Marissa Fuller. That she would put her kids first. Always. As she should. More than ever, he wanted to give her the world. The universe. The stars. But she wouldn't take anything from him, nothing more than a filet mignon dinner.

"Autry, are you anyone's daddy?" Kiera asked.

Poke. Heart. Stab. Autry turned to face the sweet five-year-old. "Nope. I don't have any children of my own."

"But you're so good at being a daddy," Kaylee said.

"He really is," Abby whispered to her sisters.

"You girls know I'm leaving town in a couple weeks. Leaving the country, actually. I fly all over the world for my job. A dad would need to be around for his kids. So that's why I'm not a dad."

"You could stay here," Kiera said. "In Rust Creek Falls."

"He can't," Abby said. "He's the president of his company."

"Oh," Kiera and Kaylee said at the same time.

The good news was that Abby understood. She didn't look sad. Or wistful.

Just as the four of them finished cleaning up the kitchen, the oven timer dinged.

"Looks like our pigs in a blanket are ready!" Autry said. "Why don't you gals head into the family room and get good seats? I'll be in in a minute."

When he was alone in the kitchen, he sucked in a breath. He and Marissa had come to the right conclusion last night. If they were romantic, they'd act romantic, and Abby, especially, would notice immediately. Suddenly she would look at him as a potential father figure instead of as a family friend. And he couldn't risk that, for the girl's sake. He cared about her and her family too much for that. He'd focus instead on being a good cowboy.

Pigs in a blanket on a platter, he brought them into the family room. Marissa's dad had made his famous three-bean dip with a side of crackers, and her mom had lime rickeys in a pitcher. Everyone loaded up their plates and cups and they sat down to watch episode two of *The Great Roundup*.

Marissa was next to Autry on the love seat. He could feel her glancing at him now and again, clearly trying to assess how he felt about Abby's comment.

"I think it was sweet," he whispered to Marissa.

"I think you're sweet," she whispered back.

He squeezed her hand and helped himself to a lime rickey, a drink he'd never had before. The lime juice, sugar and club soda concoction with its lime garnish was sweet and tart and refreshing.

"Yay, it's starting!" Abby said, her attention glued to the TV.

Just like last week, the contestants rode up to the canteen site on horseback to where the host, Jasper Ridge—once again decked out all in black—awaited. Autry recognized Brenna and Travis, the pair from Rust Creek Falls, who leaned over for a romantic kiss, which got some claps and calls to get a room from the other contestants.

"Aww, they're so in love!" Abby squealed.

Summer Knight, the rodeo star who'd made it clear she had her eye on stealing Travis from Brenna, sidled up close to him and winked at the camera. Autry wondered how much of this was staged for ratings and how much was real. It was hard to tell. From Brenna's narrowed eyes at Summer, it could be either. Travis had something of an aw-shucks look on his face, as though he couldn't help it that women were throwing themselves at him.

The first challenge involved cutting and baling hay. Travis sure was good at that. Brenna—not so much. But then again, she was a hairstylist not a cowgirl.

"Will Brenna be eliminated?" Marissa's mom asked.

"Oh, I doubt it," her dad said. "Others are doing even worse."

"I'm rooting for Brenna not to get eliminated!" Abby said.

Autry glanced around at the roomful of relatives enjoying the show over a home-cooked meal. This sure was…nice. And comfortable. He tried to imagine the Joneses ever doing something like this. Well, once in a blue moon over the years there was Thanksgiving football, but that never lasted long, since his dad would invariably get a business call and one or two of his brothers would have a date or other plans, including himself. None of them particularly wanted to hang out.

The Fuller-Rafferty clan was very lucky, and one thing he admired so much about them was that they knew it. Some folks took this kind of family closeness for granted, but this crew didn't. Maybe because they'd lost so much? Regardless, they knew what they had and they treasured it.

A chill snaked up Autry's back. In just a couple weeks he'd be gone and this would be nothing but a memory. A nice memory, at least.

As the show wound down and the girls decided who they thought would get eliminated, Autry thought about the kids competition and the events listed on the entry form. He took out his phone and started typing notes about the challenges he and Abby would practice.

"Mr. Autry, you might not know this," Abby said during a commercial break, "but our house rule is no cell phone use in the family room."

Autry glanced up at her. His family could have used that rule when he was growing up. "And it's a good rule. But I'm actually using it as a paper and pencil to come up with ideas for the challenges we should practice for. I haven't walked backward while holding a cowboy hat with a raw egg in it in a long time. Maybe even never. Probably never."

Marissa laughed. "What else was on the poster?"

"I remember a three-legged race while trying to rope a robotic calf," Abby said.

"I have a robot dog," Kiera said. "Mr. Autry gave him to me. You can use him if you want."

Abby flung her arms around her sister. "Kiera, did I ever tell you you're an awesome sister?"

Kiera grinned.

"I want to give something," Kaylee said.

"How about if we borrow your jump rope and use it for a lasso?" Abby asked.

Kaylee shrugged. "Okay."

"You're all awesome," Marissa said, smiling at her daughters.

"Roping a robotic dog while three legged," Autry said. "No problem."

The commercial ended and they all turned their attention back to the *The Great Roundup*. "Yay!" Abby cheered. "Travis won immunity! And Brenna wasn't eliminated!"

There were high fives around the room for the hometown contestants. A guy named Dean ended up getting eliminated at the end of the show.

When the show ended, Abby popped up. "Let's practice our roping skills!"

"It's late enough as it is," Marissa said. "Way past every Fuller girl's bedtime."

"Aww," the girls said in unison.

"Autry, can we practice tomorrow?" Abby asked. "Please? Pretty please with bacon on top?"

Part of him wanted to run for the hills. The other part wanted to stay with this family forever. But since he'd made a promise to Abby, coming back tomorrow and being there for the competition was as far as he had to think about right now. "You bet," he said. "We only have one week."

"Double yay!" Kiera said. "Mr. Autry will be coming over tomorrow, too!"

He glanced at Marissa, who seemed to be taking a deep breath and a step back.

You're so good at being a Daddy...

As the five-year-old's words came back to him, he knew he was the one who should be taking deep breaths and a big step in the opposite direction. But how did you do that when your heart kept you coming back, anyway?

When Autry came over the next afternoon, he noticed Marissa hanging back a bit, almost as if she was keeping watch. Assessing. Today he would focus on practicing for the competition and try to keep his eyes and thoughts off Marissa Fuller.

Ha. Like that was even possible.

Abby raced upstairs to get Kiera's remote control dog and Kaylee's jump rope, which was a bit too short, and then they all headed into the backyard. Marissa's dad got some rope and tied their two legs together. Each got a length of rope to use as a lasso, and with a little help, Autry had Abby lassoing like a pro. Well, like a nine-year-old pro.

"Okay, let the dog-calf go," Autry said.

With the robot on the move, Autry and Abby tried catching up to it, taking turns trying to lasso it. They failed miserably, mostly because they were both laughing so hard. Autry had to wipe away tears from how ridiculously funny it all was.

"Well, we might not come in first place in that challenge," Abby said, then doubled over in laughter.

Next they moved on to the raw egg in the cowboy hat while walking backward challenge, and neither dropped their eggs, so that was a plus. Tomorrow, Autry would be back to practice the hay-on-the-head challenge, where teams had to strap on a hat with a pound of hay, and whoever was fastest over the finish line with the most hay left won.

He was enjoying himself a little too much. It was time to go back to the Maverick Manor and regroup.

As he was leaving, Abby wrapped him in a hug. "You're the best, Mr. Autry."

He glanced at Marissa, who smiled warily. Her mom lifted her chin. Well, this was happening, so he'd see it through. And then he'd be in Paris. Far, far away from the Fullers. He'd miss them. That much he knew.

Later that afternoon, Marissa's dad offered to take Abby and her best friend, Janie, to Kalispell to see the movie they'd been talking about for weeks, and Marissa's mom was baking cookies with the little ones, so Marissa and her friend Anne Lattimore planned a girls' night out. A much-needed one—even if they'd both be home by eight thirty. They hadn't been able to talk in depth last week at the premiere of *The Great Roundup* at the Ace in the Hole because their table had been jammed in between others and they knew just about everyone in the bar. But tonight, episode two having aired yesterday, the Ace would be only moderately crowded.

When Marissa arrived, the Ace was only half-full. Anne sat in the back, her blond hair shining in the dim lighting. After ordering two beers and a plate of nachos with the works, the friends sat back, surveying the crowd.

"Every time someone comes into the vet's office, they ask me if I want to be fixed up with one of the five Dalton brothers," Anne said. "They're handsome, every last one of them, but I can't work up any interest in dating anyone. It's been five years since my divorce. What's my issue?"

"I think your issue looks a lot like my issue—tall, blond and blue eyed."

Anne laughed, then quickly sobered up. "Yup. I don't like to admit it. But when the boy you loved your entire life, from playing in the sandbox to high school, the boy you thought you'd marry, up and leaves town without explaining why... I guess it'll always feel unsettled."

Marissa felt for Anne. When Daniel Stockton was eighteen, his parents had died in a car accident, leaving seven children behind, most of whom were split up. Daniel had left town, breaking Anne's heart. And even though she'd married someone else, her heart had always belonged to Daniel Stockton. Autry's brother Hudson was married to Bella Stockton, one of the Stockton kids. She and her brother Jamie had been looking for their missing siblings for almost a year now.

"Sometimes I wish I could just ask him why," Anne said. "I know he was grief stricken over his parents' deaths. And I know his grandparents didn't think they had the money or the room to take in the older boys who were of age. But to just leave town? Leave his younger siblings?"

As Marissa squeezed her friend's hand, the waitress arrived with their beers and nachos. She and Anne clinked their glasses. As they did, Marissa noticed her friend's eye caught by a group of five men at the bar.

"Each of Phil Dalton's five sons is so good-looking," Anne said, upping her chin at the group of Daltons, who'd arrived in town last month with their father. Marissa noted that several single women were checking out Zach Dalton, with his longish dark hair and green eyes. "But you're right. I guess Daniel Stockton is standing between me and getting back out there. Maybe I should just start dating, force myself."

"I think you'll date when you're ready or when the right man presents himself. I certainly didn't think I was ready to date, but ever since I met Autry, it's like I'm led by my heart instead of my head. If he lived here permanently, I'd date him in a heartbeat."

"Any chance he'll stick around?"

Marissa shook her head. "He's not a small-town guy. Or a family guy. He's got Jones Holdings, Inc. in his blood and veins. Plus he's a jet-setter. He'd never be happy here."

"I've seen the way that man looks at you, Marissa. I think he'd be happy anywhere you are."

Marissa laughed and waved her hand dismissively. "In my dreams, maybe."

"To dreams, then," Anne said, and they clinked to that and dug into the nachos.

Over the next few days, Marissa kept a bit of distance between herself and Autry. He came over every day to practice with Abby, and her heart squeezed even more every time he made sure the two little Fuller girls felt included, even though they were too young to participate in the event itself. On Friday night, as Marissa was tucking Abby into bed, her daughter sat up and wrapped her in a tight hug. She hadn't had one of those from Abby in a while.

"What's that for?" Marissa asked.

"Tomorrow I'm going to feel like everyone else for the first time in a long time," Abby whispered. "You know? I mean, Janie's mom and dad are divorced, but she sees her dad all the time and he's doing The Great Roundup Kids Competition with her. And now I'll have someone standing in as *my* dad."

Marissa touched her sweet, beautiful daughter's face. "That means a lot to you, huh?"

Abby nodded, then burst into tears. "Is that wrong?"

Oh no, what was this? Marissa pulled Abby against her and gently wiped away her tears. "Why would that be wrong, sweetie?"

But fresh tears streamed down Abby's cheeks. "Because I *have* a dad. Even though he's not here anymore. He'll always be my dad. Maybe he's watching from heaven and it's hurting his feelings."

Marissa held Abby to her, stroking her dark, silky hair. "Abby, your daddy is always watching over us. And I think he'd be very touched that Mr. Autry is going to be your partner in the competition. You know why?"

"Why?"

"Because it was nice of Mr. Autry to want to be your partner. And your dad would like anyone who was kind to you and our family. Your daddy wants you to be happy, sweetheart."

Abby thought about that for a moment, then nodded. "I think so, too, Mom." She smiled and settled back down in bed, her hands around the ancient Raggedy Ann doll that had been passed down from grandmother to mother to daughter. Abby's eyes drifted closed. "'Night, Mommy."

Tears stung Marissa's eyes and she blinked them away. "Good night, my sweet girl. I love you so much."

"I love you, too."

Before she could start bawling, Marissa tiptoed out of Abby's room.

Chapter Ten

"Listen, Dad, I have to be somewhere this morning—" Autry glanced at his watch "—in five minutes. So we'll have to continue this discussion later. Or preferably not at all."

"You listen to me, Autry," his father bellowed. "I want you on that flight this morning. My admin already booked it. Just have your hotel pack your bags and be at the gate on time. End of story."

Walker Jones the Second had called every night since Alexandra had tried to lure him home, screeching up a storm about how Autry had hurt Alexandra's feelings and that she'd reported he'd chosen "some country mouse" over her and wouldn't return home with her. Autry had told his father he would finish his vacation, that he was enjoying time with his brothers and getting to know their wives and he had zero interest in Alexandra.

"If you think I'm losing you to that hick town and

some country mouse, you're wrong!" Walker the Second had shouted during last night's call.

"Dad, do you hear yourself?" Autry had asked. "And stop referring to Marissa as a country mouse. I won't stand for you insulting her."

"Ah, so the country mouse has a name," his father had said with a snort. "Marissa. She must be stacked."

Autry had hung up on Walker Jones the Second. The first time he'd ever done that.

Now, five minutes before Autry had to be at Rust Creek Falls Park for The Great Roundup Kids Competition, his father had called back, demanding to get his way—which was for Autry to fly home immediately.

Wasn't happening.

"Dad, you have an opportunity here to fix your relationship with Walker and Hudson," Autry said. "Why can't that be more important to you than business?"

"Our family and our business are synonymous," his father said. "That you don't understand that is mind-boggling."

Oh, Dad, Autry thought. *Please don't be the lost cause I'm thinking you are. Please give me hope that we can salvage this family.*

"Will you be on the plane home?" his father asked, his voice cracking. "I can't lose you, Autry. I just can't."

For the first time in maybe…ever, Autry heard anguish in his dad's voice, and it caught him off guard, to the point that he had to sit down for a second.

His head was spinning. Flashing in and out of his mind were images—his father, his mother, his four brothers at various ages. Karinna and Lulu and the nursery in his condo that he'd had someone come pack up and take to a charity. The offices at Jones Holdings,

Inc. in Tulsa. The view outside his window at Maverick Manor. The faces of the three Fuller girls, Kaylee, Kiera and Abby. And their beautiful mother, Marissa, who was no country mouse. Not that there was anything wrong with a country mouse.

He saw himself saying goodbye to them, the little girls wrapped around his legs. *"But you're like our daddy now,"* they said in unison. *"Abby said so."*

You're our daddy now. You're our daddy now...

The words echoed in his head until Autry could barely breathe.

"Autry, are you there? Can I count on you to come home today?" his father asked.

Autry didn't answer. But he didn't move, either, and he was now late for meeting Marissa and the girls.

You're our daddy now. This is what having a dad is like. I remember. It's just like this.

Just like this. Just like this...

Autry leaned back on the chair and stared out the window, unable to think, unable to move.

Abby woke up at the crack of dawn on Saturday, so excited she was practically hyperventilating, and Marissa planned on getting everyone over to Rust Creek Falls Park on the early side. But of course, Kaylee pressed an Oat Yummy in her ear, which Marissa had to carefully extract so as not to crumble it, and then Kiera stubbed her toe and sobbed for a full three minutes, and Abby, practicing walking backward while holding an egg in a cowboy hat, dropped said egg and burst into tears and had to be consoled that she wouldn't come in in last place.

Then Ralph couldn't find his lucky socks, the ones

with the Montana State University mascot, and Roberta was searching for the new tube of sunscreen she'd bought yesterday. Marissa soothed the little ones, found the socks and the sunscreen, drank two cups of strong coffee, got a decent breakfast in everyone, and finally, the Fuller-Rafferty crew was out the door and on the way to the park to meet Autry.

Autry, whose morning was nothing like Marissa's.

Autry, who didn't have to worry about crumbling Oat Yummies in small ears or getting a houseful of people out on time.

Autry, who was like a vacation in himself.

Take me away, she sang to herself with a smile, his gorgeous face floating into her mind.

As they turned the corner, they joined a crowd headed toward the park. Huge signs and banners were strung up at the entrance and the park was packed. She and Autry had made plans to meet at eight forty-five in front of the check-in table. She looked around but didn't see him. She glanced at her watch—eight forty-four. At least she wasn't late. But Autry wasn't here yet?

When her watch ticked to eight forty-five and she saw no sign of him, she stood on tiptoe and craned her neck. She saw his brothers and their wives with their extended family entering the park, but no Autry.

Eight forty-six. Eight forty-seven.

The competition began at nine sharp and Autry wasn't even here to check in.

"Mom, where's Autry?" Abby asked, looking all around.

"I'm sure he's here and just saying hi to his brothers," she said.

But she kept her eyes glued on the park entrance and he wasn't racing in.

Her stomach twisted. Had he changed his mind? Had the reality of what he'd overheard Abby saying to his sisters about how "this is what having a dad is like" scared him off? Was partnering with Abby in a dad-like team too much for him?

It better not be, she thought, anger burning in her gut. If he disappointed her child...

Autry might not have made any commitment to Marissa, but he sure as hell had made one to Abby, and there would be serious heck to pay if he let Abby down. Marissa had no idea what, but she'd let Autry Jones have it—an earful of her ire, at the least.

Eight fifty. Eight fifty-two.

Where are you? she thought, glancing around.

Abby had gone from excitedly standing on tiptoe and looking for Autry to biting her lip with an expression of sadness and worry.

"Abby, I thought you were in the competition," one of those not-so-nice girls said as she smoothed her own pinned-on entry number. She held her dad's hand, but he was busy talking to another dad behind him.

"I...I am," Abby said. "I'm just waiting for him."

"She's not in the competition," the other girl whispered. "Her father's dead."

"She asked someone to be her dad for the day," the first girl whispered back. "Oh my God, that is so sad. I'm so sorry, Abby."

Both girls made fake sad faces at Abby.

"I'm sure both of you have somewhere to be," Marissa snapped, and the girls tugged their dads' hands and walked away.

"I guess he's not coming," Abby said, tears filling her dark eyes. Her head dropped and Marissa's heart tightened.

"Not coming?" said a familiar, deep voice. "I never break a promise, Abby. Never."

Relief flooded Marissa to the point she almost fell over. Autry stood before them, slightly out of breath as though he'd run here from Maverick Manor. Or the airport.

"Autry!" Abby squealed, her face lighting up. He picked her up and swung her around, somehow managing not to bump her into the people around them.

"Sorry I'm late," he said, glancing at Marissa. "Tough call that was hard to untangle from. But I checked us in, so let's head over to the entrants' area." He handed Abby her number to pin on her shirt.

"Yay!" Abby said. "Wish us luck!"

The Fuller-Rafferty clan hugged Abby and assured her she'd do great.

Marissa was so exhausted from the emotional tailspin she'd just been through that she could barely speak. Luckily, her mother, always at the ready, handed her a foam cup of coffee from the urns the Jones family had set up for the event, along with juices and treats.

"I never break a promise," Autry whispered to Marissa, squeezing her hand. And then he was gone, running with Abby to the entrants' line.

But you will break a heart. Mine.

Abby did not drop her egg in the three-legged backward egg-in-the-Stetson competition—cowboy hats donated compliments of the Jones brothers. Luckily, that was the first event, and though they came in

fifth place—which was saying something considering that twenty-two teams were participating—Abby
was thrilled and pumped for the rest of the challenges.
They came in first in the lasso competition, beating
out a mean girl and her dad.

By the end of the three-hour event, Autry and Abby
had a third-place ribbon, which they both proudly
pinned to their T-shirts, and the entire family went to
Buffalo Bart's Wings To Go to celebrate. Autry had
arranged for Buffalo Bart to set up a wings, beer and
soda buffet in the backyard for the family and whoever Abby and the Fuller-Raffertys wanted to invite.
When Melissa's dad tried to pay, Autry mentioned he'd
already taken care of the bill. Ralph tried to cover the
tip, but Autry insisted he'd taken care of that, too. Her
father seemed quite pleased.

"He's making up for almost being late," Roberta
whispered to Marissa.

"Oh, Mom, have a wing. And try the tangy barbecue sauce."

Roberta raised an eyebrow but went off to the wings
buffet and filled her plate.

Marissa glanced over at Abby, who was standing
with her friend Janie and trying to talk and eat a wing
at the same time. Her daughter looked so breathlessly
happy that Marissa's heart pinged in her chest.

Autry was talking to his brothers and their wives by
the beer taps, and though he was smiling, she could tell
something was bothering him. Perhaps the reason he'd
been late? She hadn't had a chance to talk to him one-
on-one since he'd arrived at the park, and the yard was
so crowded she wouldn't have a chance here, either.

He caught her eye and raised his glass to her, and

she raised her soda in return. But behind his smile she definitely saw conflict and something else she couldn't put her finger on.

Maybe she'd just have to sneak over to Maverick Manor tonight and find out what it was.

As soon as he could escape the festivities, Autry was gone, back to his hotel room. He had one more week in Rust Creek Falls, and instead of enjoying some time with Marissa, he felt like someone was stabbing him in the chest with a hot poker. Constantly. His father's plea had his gut all twisted. Abby's faith in him had his gut all twisted.

Marissa's acceptance of him had his gut all twisted, too.

Someone knocked on the door, and Autry almost didn't open it. It could be Alexandra again. Or his father. Marissa. The Fuller girls. Any number of people pulling him in opposite directions.

But it was his brother Walker. He was holding a folder.

"Need your signature on these for the preliminary Thorpe Corp. meetings in Paris," Walker said. "Dad's signed, I've signed, then you, and you're all set."

Autry took the folder, his heart so heavy he wouldn't be surprised if he broke a hole in the floor and crashed to the ground.

"Something wrong?" Walker asked.

"The water. The punch. Whatever it is. It got me."

Walker looked at him as though he had four heads, then realization dawned. "Marissa got you, you mean."

"Love got me. But how? I'm immune."

Walker laughed. "I thought I was, too. Then I met Lindsay."

"I'm going to Paris," Autry said. "I want to go."

"So figure out how to have both," Walker said.

"How? How can I fly around the world every few weeks and have a relationship? A relationship with a single mother whose kids would have expectations?" Autry shook his head. "Ridiculous. I'm not cut out for fatherhood."

He knew what happened when you thought you were, when you let your heart lead you. You got kicked in the head. Kicked to the curb.

"Autry, let me give you some advice from someone who's been there, done that. Someone who was raised by the same parents you were."

Autry looked at his brother. "I'll take it."

"You can try to lie to yourself, but the truth always outs. That's just the way it is. So first, work on accepting the truth. Then let that truth decide what you do."

"What am I lying to myself about?" he asked. "I just admitted to you that I have feelings for Marissa. That her kids matter to me."

"You have feelings. Her kids matter. You like chocolate ice cream. It's a nice day outside. Autry—I'm talking about truth, not spin."

"What do you want me to say? That I love Marissa?"

"If you do. Like I said, you can try to lie to yourself, but the truth always outs. Let the truth boss you around, Autry. Not Dad. Not what happened in the past. And not how you *think* you should feel."

Autry flipped through the papers. He'd read them carefully over the past couple of days and had just been waiting for the chairman's and CEO's signatures before he signed them. He brought the stack over to the desk and signed on the dotted lines. He was going to Paris; that was never in question or doubt.

He handed the folder back to Walker.

"You'll figure it out, brother," Walker said. "I did."

How? How would he possibly figure it out? He did have strong feelings for Marissa. Her kids did matter to him. He even adored her parents. But his job meant a lot to him, too, and he loved traveling the world, negotiating and wheeling and dealing.

Somehow, grilling steaks in a small-town backyard, playing charades, teaching Kaylee and Kiera how to play soccer, making pigs in a blanket, watching reality TV with a family and practicing for The Great Roundup Kids Competition had shown him he enjoyed that, too. More than he ever thought possible.

So fine—the truth would out. It was outing right here and now. But how could the worlds coexist?

Chapter Eleven

"You certainly snagged the most eligible bachelor in Rust Creek Falls," Helen Ganley said with a scowl as she marched up to Marissa at the reception desk in the sheriff's station. Helen lived in Anne's neighborhood and was the one who complained incessantly about dog walkers allowing their "mutts to pee on the edge of my property!"

Marissa felt her cheeks burn. Naturally, her boss was in his office and had likely heard every embarrassing word. Sheriff Christensen's two new deputies, a rookie guy and the very experienced Daniella Patterson, glanced up, the rookie wiggling his eyebrows and Daniella giving Marissa a thumbs-up.

God. Did everyone know her business? Yes. They did. Because this was a small town and she herself had paraded her business all over Rust Creek Falls.

"If you are talking about Autry Jones," Marissa said in a louder voice than usual, "we are just friends."

"Sure you are, hon," Helen said. "I want to file another complaint about the lady who lets her dog pee on my lawn."

"The very edge of your lawn?" Marissa asked. "Technically, that strip is public property, Helen."

"It's still *my* lawn," the woman said. "It's very bad for the grass! It dies!"

"Well, I personally have spoken to the lady in question and she has promised not to let her dog lift its leg on your property ever again."

"Good!" Helen snapped. "Finally."

"Helen, maybe it's time you adopted a puppy," Marissa said. "I heard the animal shelter just rescued a mother dog and her month-old pups from the woods."

Helen's face fell. "I don't think I'll ever be ready for another dog." Marissa knew that Helen's beloved miniature black poodle, Chumley, had died after sixteen years together, and the woman had gotten grumpier and grumpier ever since. But underneath that brittle exterior was a softy who needed something to dote on.

"I clock out at five," Marissa said, glancing at her watch. It was four fifty. "Let's walk over and just see them. I hear they're really cute. Black-and-white."

"Black-and-white?" Helen said, her face lifting a bit. "I suppose we could take a look."

A half hour later, Helen had signed on to foster all four pups *and* the mother dog, with the intention of adopting the mom and one puppy when they were ready. Marissa had a feeling that Helen would not be complaining about anything or anyone anymore.

After a day's work and a trip to the Rust Creek Falls Animal Shelter, all Marissa wanted to do was go home and soak in a bathtub. But it was her turn to cook, and Kiera wanted to practice her reading, and Kaylee wanted to learn to count to a hundred by tens. Wasn't that what older sisters were for? She'd put Abby on that. Except Abby wanted to redecorate her room, and Marissa had promised she'd help move the desk and bed and dresser around so that her father wouldn't throw out his back.

But when Marissa arrived home, Autry had not only rearranged Abby's bedroom and had Kaylee already working on up to fifty in the counting by tens, but was sitting on the sofa with Kiera, patiently listening to her sound out a tough word, her little finger on the page, her tongue out in concentration. *"Peh-oh-pel?"*

"Pee-pul," Autry said. "That's a toughie. Some words can't really be sounded out. You just have to learn them by sight."

"Like *house*," Kaylee said. "I learned that one."

"High five!" Autry said, hand up.

Kaylee beamed and high-fived him.

"Sorry I'm late," Marissa said. "I had an errand to run."

"Actually, it's good you're late, because dinner is just about ready. Two more minutes."

He cooks. He teaches kids to read. He teaches kids to count. He rearranges furniture.

He kisses...like he means it.

"I'll come help," she said, and Autry followed her into the kitchen. "I didn't know you were coming over tonight."

"I only have a week left. I want to spend as much time with you as I can."

"As friends."

He held her gaze. "As friends."

"Thanks for everything in there," she said, gesturing toward the other room. "I was swamped at work today, then I helped Helen Ganley turn her long-time frown upside down. And I thought I had a couple heavy hours of mom duty ahead of me. But then you were here."

"Autry Jones, at your service," he said, taking a bow. His smile almost undid her, sending a jolt to her knees.

God, she loved this man.

She froze, then felt herself tremble and took a step back.

What? She loved him?

Say something, she ordered herself. *Get that thought out of your head immediately!*

"So…what's for dinner?" she asked, her heart beating so fast she was surprised he couldn't hear it.

"My world-famous meatballs and spaghetti, with garlic bread and a green salad."

She grinned. "I may faint with happiness. So will my father. And the girls."

"Marissa, I did one more thing."

"You couldn't possibly have," she said. What was there left for this man to do?

"I know I should have asked, but the opportunity presented itself right then and there and I took it."

She tilted her head.

"A friend of mine bought eight tickets to a concert for his family, but there was a conflict, so he asked if I'd like to buy them and I did. I'd like to invite your entire family to go. You, me, your parents and the girls. And since there's an extra, maybe Abby would like to invite a friend."

"A concert? What kind?"

"It's 2LOVEU," he said. "With a certain dimpled lead singer named Lyle. Did I mention a backstage pass comes along with the tickets?"

"Oh my God. Abby might pass out. But I don't know, Autry. That's kind of out of our league."

"Not mine," he said.

"Let me talk to my mom."

"Does she like 2LOVEU?" he asked.

"Everyone does. I heard her humming one of their songs while folding laundry the other day. Abby plays their album so often that the ear worm has got us all. Even Kaylee knows half the songs by heart."

"I would love to take you all. The concert is in Seattle."

"Seattle?" she said. "But—"

"Private jet and a hotel for the night—you, your parents and the girls will have a large suite with three bedrooms, and I'll have a suite down the hall. If we're going front row to a boy-band concert, we have to do it right."

She laughed. "You really are from another universe."

He held her gaze, his expression turning serious. "Except I'm right here in your kitchen, making spaghetti and meatballs."

Tears poked at her eyes and she quickly blinked them back. That was the problem. He was so close—and yet so damned far away.

And leaving in a week.

And she loved him. She loved Autry Jones.

As Marissa and her mom unloaded the dishwasher long after Autry had gone home, Marissa figured it was time to bring up the 2LOVEU concert. The conversation would go one of two ways. Either her mom would say "Oh, how generous and nice, what a wonderful family trip!" or "Absolutely not, that's too much, and setting up expectations for not only Abby but the younger girls, too."

Her eyes narrowed, her chin lifted, Roberta listened as Marissa explained the details of the big concert trip to Seattle.

"Marissa, that's very generous of him, but come on. Front-row tickets to the concert everyone is talking about. In Seattle. A private jet there. A hotel overnight. Backstage passes. This isn't us, Marissa. It's not our life. And it's not going to be our future. Autry is leaving in a week. Then life suddenly goes back to regular."

Marissa had to smile at how her mother managed to double up on what Marissa had figured she'd say. "So maybe a special once-in-a-lifetime event isn't such a terrible thing."

Her mother frowned and put the mugs in the cabinet. "I don't know, Marissa. Honestly, I'm just not sure. He's a good person, that much I know. He's genuine. He is leaving in a week, and yet he was here tonight, making spaghetti and meatballs, helping Kiera read, helping Kaylee count, rearranging Abby's bedroom furniture, going over Dad's stock picks and fixing the crazy font increase on my desktop that I couldn't figure out. He's doing everyday things. Family things. He's spent a lot of time here, Marissa, when he could have just taken you out on the town. So I can't say he's not a lovely, family-oriented person."

"He doesn't think he's family oriented," Marissa said. "It's part of the problem."

She thought about the woman who'd hurt Autry, the baby he'd lost all contact with. He'd hardened his heart against having a family for himself, against loving again, against expectations.

"For a man who came to town to visit his family and has been spending time with them and a family of three kids, two grandparents and a widowed mom, he's more family focused than he must realize."

Marissa nodded, taking out a stack of plates. "Do you think Abby will be hurt when he leaves?" she asked.

"I think Abby will be fine. Autry is kind of like Lyle from 2LOVEU to Abby. Sort of a celebrity, except she got to know this one a little. That he's leaving won't be a surprise, and you've prepared her well for that. I think it's *you* who'll be hurt."

Chapter Twelve

"AHHH!" four little girls—three Fullers and a Lattimore—shrieked as the Jones Holdings, Inc. corporate jet cleared the cloud cover and the Seattle skyline came into view. Ever since Marissa had told her daughters about the concert and the trip to Seattle, they'd been squealing and jumping up and down and happily shrieking in anticipation. They'd also already written Autry five thank-you cards each.

"Almost there!" Autry said.

Marissa, with Kaylee and Kiera seated between her and Autry, looked out the window. She'd never been to Seattle. She'd been out of Montana only once, come to think of it. But Autry Jones probably couldn't think of a city, state or country he hadn't been to.

This is a fairy tale and then this corporate jet will turn back into a pumpkin, aka my twelve-year-old car that needs new brake pads.

For tonight, she'd take the fairy tale. In a few days,

Autry would be flying off to Paris, and then life would go back to normal.

When the plane touched down, Abby and her best friend, Janie, started clapping and singing "Only You," one of their favorite 2LOVEU songs. Even Grandpa joined in, making everyone laugh when he knew the chorus, even if he was completely off-key.

By the time they arrived at their hotel, via a private car that had met them at baggage claim, Marissa was as starry-eyed as her daughters. The hotel was right across the street from the concert venue, and had an amazing fountain across both sides of the entrance. The Fuller-Raffertys craned their necks to look up at how high the skyscraper went—maybe forty floors. The lobby was as grand as the outside—marble floors and exquisite rugs and paintings and plush couches and chairs. Marissa counted two bars and two restaurants.

Autry took care of checking in and then they were going up in the express elevator to the twenty-eighth floor.

"I'm in this room," Autry said, as he walked past room 2802. "And I booked this three-bedroom suite a few doors down for you," he added, stopping in front of room 2810. He opened the door and they all gasped.

Wow. An entire wall of windows offered an expansive view of Seattle, including the famed Space Needle. A seating area of two sofas surrounded an entertainment center, and there was a desk and kitchenette. Three doors opened to three bedrooms. Two had king-size beds and one had four twin beds.

Each bedroom had its own private bathroom—of course—with fluffy white bathrobes, including kid-size ones for the girls, and slippers.

"Oh, is this going to be nice," Roberta said, smiling as she looked around the suite.

"Told you," Ralph whispered.

As the girls went racing into their room, flinging their overnight bags on their beds and pulling out the one stuffed animal that each was allowed to bring, Marissa smiled at Autry.

"Thank you," she said. "We needed this. All of us."

"I needed it, too. I just didn't know it until I met you."

She squeezed his hand, but really wanted to fling herself into his arms and kiss him.

"So who's hungry?" Autry asked. "We have an hour before the concert starts."

"Lines at the food stands can get pretty long," Ralph said. "We'd better head over now. A hot dog with the works for me!"

"And me!" Abby said.

"Can I have a corn dog?" Kiera asked.

Kaylee wrinkled her nose. "I just want a plain hot dog."

"Hot dogs?" Autry said, scratching his chin. "Sorry, guys. But I'm not sure if they're serving that to the fifty superfans who get to dine with the band backstage before the concert."

"What?" Abby shouted, tears streaming down her cheeks. "Ahhh!" She was jumping up and down and laughing and crying with her friend and sisters.

"Oh, Autry," Marissa said. "I should have figured."

He smiled. "Always figure."

"I'm learning."

"And who says money can't buy happiness?" Autry whispered.

Marissa glanced at him and could see that even he knew it couldn't. Because even though they had tonight, all the money in the world couldn't buy a fix for what stood in the way of their happiness.

Autry, surrounded by tens of thousands of squealing, screaming, shrieking girls of all ages, almost wished he'd brought earplugs. But after a while, even he got into the boy-band music and enjoyed the show, which came complete with pyrotechnics and choreographed dances and three encores. Abby had vowed she'd never wash her right hand again after Lyle, the lead singer, shook it when they met during the superfan dinner. She was speechless when he said hi and told her he liked her sparkly green hair band, and when she shrieked, he seemed very used to it.

About an hour in, Kaylee started showing signs of tiring. The music was just too loud for her, so Marissa's parents took her back to the hotel. Autry could tell they were ready to make their escape.

When the concert ended, Abby flung herself into Autry's arms. "I'll never forget this. Never in a million years, no matter what happens in my life. I'll always have this."

He hugged her tight and glanced at Marissa, and could see tears glistening her eyes. Her daughter's happiness meant so much to her, and he'd been glad to make this special night happen for and her bestie.

Five-year-old Kiera had managed to fall fast asleep, so Marissa was about to scoop her up from her seat when Autry did instead, easily picking up the girl and cradling her against him. Kiera didn't even stir. He looked down at the sleeping angel in his arms, and the old ache poked at his heart and gut. Once, he'd thought this would be his life. But he knew better now. Things didn't last. People changed, feelings changed, and the woman looking at him with such tenderness in her expression could slam a door in his face three months from now. A virtual door, since he'd still be in Europe in three months, but still… If he cracked open his heart even just a sliver and let these people in, really in, one day he'd wake up and find them gone, and in their place would be a gnawing void. Just the way it was when Karinna had dumped him and he'd lost Lulu.

The sooner he got back to the hotel and into his own suite, the better. Carefully holding Kiera, he headed into the aisle with the throngs of others, keeping Marissa, Abby and Janie in his sights. Kiera shifted and sighed, off in dreamland, and he couldn't help a little smile, despite how off balance he felt.

"Good job, Dad," said a man who was leaving with his daughter.

"No, I—" Autry started to say, then didn't bother correcting the guy.

Dad.

He was no one's dad and would never be. Couldn't be.

As Abby and Janie chattered on excitedly about every moment of the flight, the hotel rooms, the superfan dinner and the concert itself, Marissa glanced at Autry carrying Kiera. For all anyone knew, they were a family. A mom, a dad and their three daughters leaving the concert.

For a moment, she relished how it felt to be a full unit, even just in appearance. She hadn't realized how much she'd missed that, walking to the park with Mike and the girls, a family. But the past two years, one very important family member had been gone.

She glanced at Autry again, slightly rocking Kiera as he walked, smiling now and then at Abby and Janie's conversation, now focused on how cute Lyle, the lead singer of 2LOVEU, was and how neither of them were ever washing their right hands again, no matter what, unless their moms made them.

Marissa smiled.

They looked like a typical happy family. And as Marissa realized how much she wished they could really be one, her heart started beating really fast. She loved this man. And she'd have to let him go in just a few days.

Back in the hotel suite, Autry gently put Kiera on her bed, and Marissa tucked her in, careful not to wake Kaylee, who was fast asleep, her arm around her stuffed monkey.

Abby and Janie were both still too wired from the concert to head to bed, so Grandma and Grandpa let them talk their ears off about the parts of the concert they'd missed.

"Well, I'd better let you all settle down to bed," Autry said, heading to the door.

Abby and Janie both raced over to thank him profusely and hug him, and he seemed truly touched by their gratitude.

"You're very welcome, girls. It was my pleasure," he said.

When the girls ran into their room to change into the concert T-shirts Autry had bought all the kids, Marissa went to the door, wishing she didn't have to say goodbye for the evening. She didn't want him to go, didn't want to stop looking at that handsome, kind face, didn't want to stop being in his presence, which calmed her, comforted her and yet made her feel things she hadn't even thought about in years. Excitement. Romance. Sex.

Roberta got up, and as she passed them on the way to her bedroom, she said, "Why don't you two go have a nightcap at one of those fancy bars downstairs? It's time for bed for little ones and grandparents, but you two go enjoy yourselves. No need to rush back. Dad and I will hold down the fort."

Marissa almost gasped. Was her mother actually engineering a little one-on-one time with Autry involving alcohol and a hotel? It sure seemed that way. Or perhaps her mother was just wanting the two of them to get some time to themselves, since they'd been surrounded by shrieking kids for so many hours.

"I think that's a great idea," Autry said, extending his arm.

"Thanks, Mom," she whispered and took Autry's elbow.

"I keep expecting to have to cover my ears to escape a shrill scream of joy over a cute band member leaping onstage or something," Marissa said as they rode the elevator down.

He laughed. "I know. Sometimes I realize I'm talking too loud because I've been shouting to be heard for the past three hours." He leaned close and whispered, "Is this too loud?"

Every nerve ending in her body tingled. "No, that's just right."

She held on to his arm and he led the way to Bar 22.

It was elegant, low lit, with club chairs and couches and secluded corners. They chose a plush velvet love seat in one of those spots meant for two, and a sleek waiter appeared to take their orders.

"I don't feel dressed up enough for this place," Marissa said, glancing around at the women in cocktail dresses or stylish casual clothes. She was in a silky tank top and jeans, a light cardigan sweater tied around her waist, her usual silver ballet flats on her feet and her hair loose around her shoulders. In other words, dressed just right for the Ace in the Hole or a teeny-bopper concert.

"You look perfect and beautiful as always, Marissa," he said. "And I mean that."

She reached up to touch his face before she could think about it or stop herself. He so often said exactly the right thing, the thing that slipped inside her heart and kept adding check marks in the pro-Autry column. The con column had only one check mark in it: for the fact that he was leaving in a few days. There'd been another, the little business of him being from a completely different world, where private jets and super-fan dinners with the most popular band in America were no biggie, but Autry didn't act like he was from another galaxy. He acted like a regular person. Someone she could love. Someone she did love.

Someone who would poof away with all the magic, leaving her as Cinderella, but without a missing glass slipper. He would go his way and she would go hers, and they'd have their memories, but that would be that.

Marissa sipped her red wine. "Autry, I know I've said it quite a few times tonight, but I have to say it

again. Thank you. For a perfect evening. For making
my family so happy."

"What about you, though, Marissa? What would
make you happy?"

"When my crew is happy, I'm happy." She smiled.
"I guess it's hard to separate one from the other. It's
been a long time since it's been just me, you know?"

He didn't challenge her, didn't keep asking, didn't
push, and she could tell from the way he was looking
at her that he was thinking about what would make
him happy right then. To be upstairs in bed with her.

Which made *her* happy.

Oh God. She just realized that having sex with
Autry Jones would indeed make her happy. It might
break her heart later, but now, right now, she wanted
nothing more. And later, she'd have her memories. Yes,
she thought. Why shouldn't she allow herself just one
night with Autry Jones? A perfect night to wrap up a
perfect evening. Today was a fairy tale and it would
end happily. Tomorrow she'd be back home, back in
her regular life, looking for lost light-up sneakers and
pulling Oat Yummies out of ears and doing load after
load of laundry.

But while mopping the kitchen floor or scrubbing
the upstairs bathroom, she could see herself stopping
to think about her one perfect night with Autry, and
the magic of it would sustain her.

Was she rationalizing? Maybe. But so be it. She was
a grown woman.

"What would make me happy?" She paused and
looked at him, and she was pretty sure her answer was
written all over her face.

He sucked in a breath and leaned close and kissed

her. She kissed him back, grateful for their secluded corner.

"Just for tonight," she said.

"Just for tonight."

She kissed him again, her hands on his face, everything she felt going into the fierce kiss. "No strings attached," she whispered.

"That's always been the case," he said.

No strings. She'd shake on that again, but not on being friends. She couldn't be casual friends with Autry, not after this and certainly not after they made love.

"Maybe we should take this conversation upstairs," he said.

"I think we're done talking," she whispered and kissed him again.

They kissed all the way upstairs, prompting one giggled "get a room" from a couple entering the elevator as they exited.

Please let this night happen, he prayed to the universe. They'd been interrupted once before, in his room at Maverick Manor, and he figured he'd never have the chance again to have Marissa Fuller to himself, to explore every morsel of her amazing body, to show her just how much he wanted her.

"Shhh," Marissa whispered, her finger against her lips as they headed to Autry's room, which was thankfully several doors down from the Fuller-Rafferty clan's.

He smiled and unlocked the door, then kissed her inside, shutting the door behind them with his back. She unbuttoned his shirt and he let it fall to the floor.

As she undid his belt buckle, he sucked in a breath, barely able to stop himself from taking her right there on the probably-not-that-soft-on-the-back carpet.

The belt joined the shirt. All she'd taken off were her shoes.

They stood in front of the wall of windows, the Seattle city view barely visible through the filmy curtain. He liked that the lighting was dim in the room, romantic, but that he was able to see her. He wanted to see everything.

He slid off her silky tank top, his gaze rooted to the lacy white bra she wore. He let his hands explore her bare skin, her smooth stomach and sexy waist, and then he slid a finger underneath the straps of her bra and slid it down so he could savor every bit of skin as her beautiful breasts were revealed to him. His legs slightly buckled and he focused on unclasping the bra to keep himself from exploding—literally and figuratively.

He knelt in front of her and pulled down the zipper of her jeans, wriggling them off her sexy hips. *Mmm*, he thought, at the sight of the white cotton underwear. So damned sexy he again had to fight for control, counting to five in his head.

He picked her up and carried her into the bedroom and laid her on the bed, getting rid of his own jeans right afterward. He covered her body with his, tiny scraps of cotton and lace separating them. She kissed him passionately, her hands in his hair, and he couldn't wait another moment. He wriggled down her panties with a finger on each hip, his mouth exploring hers, then her neck, then her breasts, then her stomach and lower until she gasped and gripped the sides of the comforter. She let out a moan and he smiled.

When he felt her own hands on his hips, the boxer briefs sliding down, her cool, soft fingers touching him, he again had to count to five, then ten, to keep control.

Finally he ran out of numbers. He quickly put on a condom and then in moments was making love to Marissa, each thrust underscoring how much he wanted her, how badly he needed her, how deeply he loved her.

Oh hell.

There it was. He loved Marissa Fuller.

Shut up, Jones, he told himself. *Just lose yourself in this night.*

He took his own advice and pulled Marissa on top of him, reveling in the gorgeous sight of her naked, an expression of pleasure rippling across her face.

Finally, there was an explosion of sensation and Autry was gone, gone, gone into it, unable to think of anything but release and Marissa.

He pulled her close against him and trailed a finger down her cheek. "That was amazing. *You* are amazing."

"That was pretty damned amazing," she agreed, laughing between breaths, her hand entwined with his.

"Stay the night," he whispered.

"I wish I could. But I can't. You know I can't." She turned on her side to face him. "Thank you for this magical night, Autry Jones. Every last moment of it."

That sounded like goodbye. A final goodbye.

But they had a few more days. He couldn't bear to be in Rust Creek Falls and not see Marissa. But he was leaving. Love or not, he was getting on that plane to Paris.

You had no business getting involved with a single mother. With three kids.

But he had. And he didn't know which was scarier. That he loved her and the girls...or the idea of letting Marissa go.

Chapter Thirteen

In Autry style, he treated the group to breakfast in the hotel restaurant. Ralph was so surprised to see the size of his bacon, Swiss and tomato omelet that he took a photo of it, and Abby and Janie tried to teach him to how to upload it on social media. But of course, Ralph didn't have any social media accounts.

They ate, they drank their six-dollar glasses of orange juice and four-dollar cups of coffee, and then they were on the corporate jet again, flying back to real life.

This time, Marissa sat next to her mom, the two little Fuller girls across the aisle like "big girls" with their headphones on as they watched *Frozen* for the hundredth time. Abby and Janie also had their headphones on, but they were listening to 2LOVEU on their tiny iPod shuffles, Christmas gifts from Marissa and Anne last year.

Autry was a few rows up, next to her father, chatting about the stock market. Every now and then, Autry would turn and Marissa would get a glimpse of his beautiful profile, his strong, straight nose, that sculpted jawline and the sexy sweep of dark blond hair.

She sighed before she could catch herself.

"What was that for?" her mother whispered.

"What? Nothing. Just…a little tired."

"Uh-huh," Roberta said, eyebrow raised. "Maybe I was wrong, honey," she added. "Maybe playing it safe isn't the way to go."

"Of course it is," Marissa whispered. "That's the only way *to* go."

"But you're not escaping without a bruised heart."

"I also need to be realistic. He's who he is. I'm who I am. Our lives can't meet, Mom. How could they?"

Even that one had Roberta stumped.

"Autry loves what he does. He loves traveling for his family business. He might have very strong feelings for me, for all of us, but let's say he mysteriously and magically said he's going to stay in Rust Creek Falls for me. He'd be miserable. I know that and so does he."

Roberta covered Marissa's hand. "I guess so. Well, I have no doubt the two of you will figure it out."

"Or not," Marissa said, tears poking her eyes. "You know that annoying saying 'it is what it is'? Well, it is what it is."

"It's okay to admit that you're going to miss him," Roberta said. "And it's okay to be sad."

Marissa felt tears stir again. "It's not, though. I have the girls to think about. I have to be strong for them. Present for them. One of the reasons I don't date is so that I won't bring my crazy emotions into their lives. They lost so much. I just want to focus on raising them well and making sure they're happy."

"You're a good mother, Marissa."

"You taught me well."

Her mother pulled Marissa into a hug, as much as she could, given that they were buckled in.

"But you deserve happiness, too, sweetheart. Just don't forget that."

Marissa nodded and closed her eyes, but there was no way she'd sleep. She'd taken her ounce of happiness last night and it would keep her going through the lonely times, through the times she'd miss Autry. She had her girls. She had her parents. She had friends and a good job. She had a life in Rust Creek Falls and it was a good one.

She'd let Autry go because she had to.

Autry dropped off Janie first, Anne Lattimore ran to hug her daughter and thank everyone for taking her on the amazing adventure. Then the car headed to the Fuller-Raffertys', and Marissa wondered if this was the last time she'd see Autry, if this would be their final goodbye. She knew he'd never leave town without saying goodbye to the girls, but this was likely Marissa's last time alone with Autry.

Her parents ushered the kids inside, Roberta ensuring that Marissa had some time alone with Autry to say that goodbye, if that was what she wanted. It wasn't, but why prolong this for three more days?

"I can't be here in this town and stay away," Autry said as soon as they were alone, his hands gripping the leather steering wheel of his rented Porsche.

"There's no future for us," she said.

"I could fly in every few months and…" He sighed.

"This was supposed to be no strings attached, but we forgot that feelings are strings," he added.

She smiled and reached for his hand. "I know. So let's just cut them now. I need to take care of my family, Autry. I can't be lying in my bed, nursing a broken heart. I don't have that luxury."

"I know. Well, we have three more days. What's three more days of exquisite torture? It would be worse not seeing each other when I'm still here, Marissa."

Now it was her turn to sigh as her resolve went out the window. "Agreed."

"Your parents were champs during this trip. Let's give them a night out tonight. Send them to dinner and a movie. I'll cook for you and the girls and we'll play board games and charades."

"Now, that sounds like my life," she said.

"A life I want to be part of while I'm here."

"See you later, then, Autry Jones."

She could see the relief on his face that she hadn't said goodbye. But she had no idea if she was doing the right thing.

"Yay! Mr. Autry is here!" Kiera said when he arrived. She was standing in the doorway with her sisters.

He laughed. These girls had a way of making him feel like a rock star. "Yay! Kiera is here! And Kaylee! And Abby!" He growled like a bear and bent over, then charged in, scooping up each girl for a hug and kiss.

Good God, what was with him? One minute he was having arrows shot in his heart from the reminders of Lulu. The next minute, he had a three-year-old on his shoulders singing a song from *Frozen*.

Who was he turning into? *What* was he turning into?

It got me. And it's gonna get you, too... He remembered his brother Hudson's words. His brother Walker's words.

And his father's. *I can't lose you, too.*

As he headed into the kitchen with his grocery bag, he thought about the fact that he didn't want to lose himself, either. He knew who he was when he was doing things Autry Jones did. Bringing over gifts. Flying off to front-row seats to a sold-out concert. But this more homespun stuff, nice as it was, left him feeling just a bit...uncomfortable.

Maybe that was a sign. That he didn't have to worry about leaving his heart in Rust Creek Falls. Tonight was definitely a good idea. He'd have another "family" night, and he'd be itching to get to Paris, to trade his cowboy boots for his five-hundred-dollar leather Prada shoes. Though he'd been here at the Fuller-Raffertys', grilling, playing charades, practicing for The Great Roundup Kids Competition, and he'd had a great time.

Cripes.

"I thought I heard shrieks of happiness," Marissa said, coming into the kitchen. "I knew a celeb had arrived."

"They certainly make me feel that way," he said, pulling out a package of thin-sliced chicken breasts and four sweet potatoes. "I'm making my world-famous chicken fingers with honey-mustard dipping sauce and sweet potato fries."

"Yum. Sounds delicious. Need an assistant?"

"I've got this. Go relax."

As Marissa left, her father came in. "I hear I owe you one. Dinner and a movie? I could get used to this.

And luckily, the only good movie out right now is an action flick, so it's my night."

Autry laughed. "Have a great time."

When Marissa's father left, Autry got to work, grabbing what he needed from the cupboards. As he turned to the refrigerator, he was drawn to a photo of Marissa and a baby who had to be Abby. Marissa looked all of sixteen, but she must have been eighteen. Man, she was young. A mother since eighteen. Her entire adult life. And here he was, thirty-three and completely unencumbered, except for the way he felt.

There were family photos and colorful drawings all over the refrigerator and magnets holding reminder cards for dentist appointments and the water bill. This was home life. Family life.

The opposite of Autry's life. On his refrigerator door at his Tulsa condo? Nothing. Not much in it, either, since he was rarely there.

"Autry!" Marissa came rushing into the kitchen, a worried look on her face. "My friend Suzanne's fiancé just ended their engagement. She's beside herself. I need to go over there. Can you watch the girls? Or I could call my parents and have them come back."

He shook his head. "Don't you dare. Just go. Take all the time she needs. I've got this."

"You sure?"

"Completely. Go."

She threw her arms around him and whispered "thank you" in his ear, sending his pulse racing at the reminder of what she'd whispered in his ear last night.

Last night now seemed a million nights ago.

He heard Marissa telling the girls that Mr. Autry was in charge and they were to listen to him, be polite and behave themselves. Then he heard the front door close.

Three heads poked in the kitchen door. "Can we help?" Abby asked.

"Well, I'm actually looking for three assistants," Autry said. "Would any of you like the job?"

"Me!" three voices said, three hands shooting up and waving frantically.

"Perfect. You're all hired," he said.

Luckily, Abby reminded her sisters to wash their hands, because he wouldn't have thought of it. The two little Fullers took turns on the step stool, and then looked to him for instructions. *Ha.* If only they knew that he'd been busy on his laptop before coming over, looking up recipes and watching two cooking videos.

He put Abby on egg-cracking duty. Kiera was in charge of shaking the seasoned bread crumbs on a plate. And Kaylee's job was to put the chicken breasts in the egg wash.

Sixteen chicken fingers were created without a single one dropping on the floor or egg wash getting in anyone's eyes or hair. Granted, Kiera had bread crumbs in her hair, but all in all, it was a perfect cooking experience. He had Abby rinse the sweet potatoes and then he sliced them, and had Kiera brush them with olive oil and Kaylee sprinkle them with salt. Then everything went into the oven, and Autry and the girls headed into the family room.

"Want me to teach you the lyrics to 'Only You'?" Abby asked as Autry settled on the couch, the three girls on beanbags.

"What makes you think I don't know them?" he asked with a grin. "Okay, fine, I know one line of the chorus.

'I'd travel to the ends of the earth for you-oo-oo,'" he sang, and the girls clapped, then started singing the rest of the song.

If his brothers could see him now. If his father could see him now. Autry had tried to put his dad out of his mind since their phone conversation the morning of The Great Roundup Kids Competition. Autry had promised nothing, but had made it clear he was staying in Rust Creek Falls until his flight left for Paris.

Just don't get married. For the love of Pete.

Autry had laughed, which had made his father feel better. Autry. Married. Come on.

Except it wasn't funny—that his father was pushing the single life, or at least the single life until Autry was back in his own territory. Walker Jones the Second really and truly didn't care if his sons were happy. And that was damned sad.

After the singalong, Abby got out Chutes and Ladders and they played a round—Kiera won—and then they played charades. The Fuller girls acted out the band 2LOVEU, which Autry would never in a million years have guessed correctly before last night.

Then it was time for dinner, so the girls went into the dining room and Autry served his chicken fingers and fries, which were a hit, even if Kaylee didn't like the honey-mustard sauce and Kiera didn't like the sweet potato fries.

"So, let's do our share," Abby said. "You first, Kaylee."

Kaylee put down her fork. "I'll share that I got to go on a plane two times."

"Me, too!" Kiera said. "That was my share. Oh,

wait. I have another. I got to go to the 2LOVEU concert yesterday! It was awesome!"

"Hey, that was my share," Abby said with a grin.
"But I have another. I have a few big dreams. One can't
come true. Ever. I didn't think the others would, either,
because they just seemed impossible. But I got to meet
Lyle from 2LOVEU. I got to shake his hand. He actually looked at me and told me it was nice to meet me."
She burst into tears. "That was the happiest moment
of my entire life."

Autry froze for a moment. "Are those happy tears?"

Abby laughed even though fresh tears were rolling
down her cheeks. "Yes! First I got to be in The Great
Roundup Kids Competition even though I don't have
a dad. And then I got to meet Lyle. How could two
dreams come true in a week?"

"Because Mr. Autry is magic," Kiera said. "Remember, that's what Kaylee said when she first told him
about us. He did magic tricks."

Autry smiled. He was magic for this family. It was
a good reminder that this wasn't real—this being-the-
family-man thing. Yeah, he was here. Doing it. But
it was temporary. And while this might be everyday
life for the Fuller girls, this was magic to him. This
house, this dinner, this conversation with these children. Magic.

After dinner they settled back in the family room to
watch the third episode of *The Great Roundup*, which
he was recording so Marissa could watch it later or
tomorrow. He wanted to shield three sets of little eyes
when Summer Knight, rodeo star, rode into the canteen in a push-up bra and a very low-cut tank top. She
flirted with Travis, who had an aw-shucks type of re

sponse to her, which had Brenna leaping into action to keep her man away from "that woman."

Autry glanced over at Kaylee and realized she'd fallen asleep on her beanbag chair just twenty minutes in. Ten minutes later, Kiera was out. Autry covered them with throws.

"Just us left," he said to Abby, who was curled up on her own beanbag and munching on the popcorn he'd made in the hot-air popper.

Abby grinned, then her smile faded. "Autry?"

"Yup," he said.

"Are you and my mom a couple?"

It was a good thing he wasn't eating popcorn right then because he would have choked.

He didn't know if he should be saying anything. This seemed a subject Marissa should handle, to answer Abby's questions as she saw fit.

"I adore your mom. And the three of you. But I'm leaving for Paris this Saturday. And I'll be there for at least a year, maybe longer. My company will be buying a big corporation there and I'll be running it and looking into other businesses in Paris to add to our company's holdings."

"Can't you start a company here?" she asked. "Janie said she heard her mom talking and that your brother Walker did that. Now he lives here. You could do the same."

Oh hell. Now he was in trouble. "Well, Walker and I do different things for our family company. I'm the brother that flies all around the world and checks out new businesses we could invest in or buy."

"Oh," she said. "That does sound fun, flying all over the world. I was looking at 2LOVEU's world tour and they're going everywhere in six months." Her face lit up. "And just think, I got to see them while they were still in our country!"

"I'm really glad you had a great time, Abby."

The brightness dimmed a little. "Thanks, Mr. Autry. For everything."

Dammit, now it sounded like a nine-year-old was saying goodbye. She was too wise for her years.

The show ended, and Autry turned to Abby. "So what's next? A movie? We can make this a double feature."

"Ooh, can we watch *Brave*?" she asked.

"*Brave* it is," he said, finding it in their cable lineup.

They settled back to watch, and Autry was surprised to find himself liking the animated film.

"Ooh, this is my favorite part," Abby said, munching on the popcorn as she turned her attention to the TV and didn't make a peep for the next hour.

Saved by *Brave*. The irony wasn't lost on Autry. He was far from courageous. He didn't know how much more of the conversation he could handle.

He glanced at Abby's sisters, sleeping so peacefully on their beanbags, and felt his heart expand.

Which had to be his imagination. He'd seen *The Grinch That Stole Christmas* every year of his childhood. He wasn't a grinch, but he had let his heart shrink to barely nothing.

Until he came to Rust Creek Falls and met this family. This family that made him want to be what they needed.

He couldn't be the dad they needed. That was out of the question. He could handle a few hours here and there, but he was never opening the floodgates again.

He'd done that and got slammed against a brick wall, to be left bruised and battered. A little bit of playing house was one thing. Really doing it? Quite another.

That debate settled in his head—and what was left of his heart—Autry sat back and watched the animated movie heroine show a lot more moxie than he'd ever have.

When the movie ended, Abby was yawning like crazy. He carried Kaylee and then Kiera up to bed, tucking them in, his heart boomeranging all over the place. Kaylee curled up on her side and grabbed hold of her stuffed monkey. Kiera's little pink mouth hung open and one arm was flung dramatically over her head, and she looked so darned cute that he wanted to take a picture for Marissa, but figured the flash would wake her.

Then he walked Abby up to her room. She'd already taped the new 2LOVEU poster on her wall, this one featuring only Lyle.

"Isn't he just the best?" Abby said as she got into bed, pulling the covers up.

He sat down on the stool beside her bed and glanced up at Lyle with his dimples. "Seems that way."

Abby sat up. "Actually, I'd say there's a tie now. You're both the best with me." She held out her arms and he hugged her, barely able to breathe. Figuratively.

"That means a lot, Abby," he said, standing up. "Sweet dreams, kiddo."

"Autry?"

He turned back. Abby was lying on her side, her eyes closed, her arms around what looked like an ancient Raggedy Ann doll. "Thanks for making me remember what it's like to have a dad. It sure is nice."

He froze, unsure what to say, what to do. From Abby's steady breathing, it was clear she'd already fallen asleep.

He'd barely made it downstairs before he felt his collar tightening around his neck. He needed to get some air, but he couldn't leave because he was babysitting someone's children.

Autry Jones babysitting children. Reminding a nine-year-old girl what it was like to have a father.

I can't handle that kind of responsibility for a kid's feelings, he thought, something shuttering over his heart.

Abby had said something like that before—to her sisters. But somehow it felt different when she said it to him. As if she had expectations. As if he would hurt her by not fulfilling that role.

Stop it, he ordered himself. *She didn't say you had to be her father. She just said you reminded her what it's like to have a dad. And that it was nice.*

He sure wouldn't know.

A coldness settled around him, and he sat down in the kitchen with a cup of black coffee. The minute Marissa got home, he'd be out of there.

Marissa reluctantly left Suzanne's apartment over the drugstore once her friend's two sisters had driven in from Kalispell. Poor Suzanne. She'd been with her fiancé, Jared, for two years, and had only recently gotten engaged. They almost hadn't, because Jared could not and would not say that he wanted children, and Suzanne wanted at least two, though she'd settle for one. Jared didn't commit to that until Suzanne had said that maybe they wouldn't be happy together. So he had finally said the magic words: "One child sounds all right. Let's get married."

And now he'd admitted he really didn't mean it and just hadn't wanted to lose Suzanne. So she was in love with a man who didn't want something she wanted— a fundamental difference that had torn them apart.

Marissa couldn't help thinking of herself and Autry. A man who might have strong feelings for her, who might even love her, unless she was reading way too much into the way he looked at her, the way he held her when and after they'd made love in the Seattle hotel. But a man who didn't want to be a family guy, who didn't want a family, who'd closed his heart to family. A man who lived to travel and loved to travel.

A man whose life was at odds with hers.

She'd known this three weeks ago when they'd met at the Ace in the Hole. And she'd gone and fallen for the guy, anyway.

"Marissa!"

Marissa turned around. Helen Ganley, the woman who'd taken on the mama dog and her four puppies as fosters, was crossing the street with the mother dog on a leash.

Oh no. Was Helen going to complain again about the lady who let her dog pee on the edge of her lawn? Marissa had hoped that adopting a dog herself would open the woman's heart a little.

"Maria here is doing just great," Helen said, giving the pretty black-and-white dog a pat on the head and a little dog treat from her pocket. "I wanted to thank you, Marissa. You suggested I adopt a dog and you were right. Maria and her puppies changed my life."

"Aww, I'm so glad, Helen. She's a beauty." Marissa

scratched Maria behind the ears. She thought Maria was a fine name for a pretty dog.

"And I should thank that big fish you caught," Helen added. "It's thanks to him that Maria and her pups got saved at all."

Huh? What did Autry have to do with it? Her expression must have asked the question because Helen said, "Oh, I'm not surprised he didn't mention it. The most generous people rarely toot their own horns. Two week ago, Autry Jones donated a small fortune to the Rust Creek Falls Animal Shelter and that's how the shelter was able to buy more kennels and supplies. They're going to expand even more now. I also heard he started a fund with the PTO for programs for students with 'homes in transition,' meaning those who've lost a parent or whose folks are separated or divorced."

Marissa sucked in a breath. "He did?"

"That's what I heard. My sister-in-law is the PTO president—that's how I know. Don't let him get away, Marissa. I'm a widow myself and I was alone too long. Then my darling Chumley died and turned me grumpy. All it took was something—five new somethings—to love and care for, and I was back in business."

Marissa smiled. "I'm so happy to hear that, Helen."

As her neighbor continued down the street with Maria, Marissa couldn't move. Autry had donated to the animal shelter? He'd started a fund for school programs for students who'd experienced the death of a parent, or divorce? How much more wonderful could Autry be?

She got her legs to move and headed home. When she opened the front door, the house was quiet. Autry was in the kitchen, putting away the clean dishes from the dishwasher, and the room was spotless.

"Hey," she said. "Mr. Mom."

He barely smiled.

She bit her lip. "Everything go okay?"

He put the last plate away, then ran a hand through that thick, silky hair of his. "Everything went great. The girls are all asleep in their rooms. Kaylee and Kiera conked out pretty early, but Abby taught me the lyrics to every 2LOVEU song off the new album. Oh, and Kaylee doesn't like honey-mustard sauce and Kiera doesn't like sweet potatoes."

Marissa was so overcome with emotion that she rushed to throw her arms around him. "You're wonderful. Just wonderful. I'm very thankful I met you, Autry Jones, even though you're leaving in two days."

He gave her a quick hug, but then stepped back. "Me, too. It was a honor spending time with you and your girls." He glanced at his watch. "Well, I'd better get to the Manor. I have some papers to go over before a meeting with Walker in the morning."

Oh. Disappointment flooded her. She'd thought maybe he'd stay a bit longer and they could have coffee or some wine, talk for a little while. But he clearly wanted to leave. Maybe a few hours with the Fuller girls had shown him exactly what he already knew: that he wouldn't be up for this full-time.

She wrapped her arms around herself as a chill settled around her. If she was this affected by his leaving for the night, how was she going to feel when he left for *good*?

Chapter Fourteen

After tossing and turning all night, Autry stayed in bed longer than he normally would, then remembered he had a meeting with Walker at ten. The thought perked him up some; talking business with Walker was standard stuff, regular life—as opposed to his evening of babysitting Marissa's daughters. He hated how standoffish he'd been with Marissa when she'd gotten home last night. She deserved better treatment than that, but he'd had to get out there, had to breathe.

He got out of bed and took a long, hot shower, then had two strong cups of coffee. By nine forty-five he'd shaken off thoughts of last night and was completely focused on business and the upcoming Thorpe Corp. negotiations.

His phone beeped with a text. It was Walker. Meet me at Just Us Kids instead of home.

Oh hell. Kiddie central again.

He walked over to the day care, reminded of the first

day he'd arrived in Rust Creek Falls and had stood in this spot on the sidewalk, practically hyperventilating about having to go inside. Well, at least he could walk in calmly, like a normal person who wasn't scared spit-less of little humans.

This time, Just Us Kids was a lot more crowded. A long table held a bunch of toddlers who were making something out of clay. On the far side of the room, a teacher was reading aloud to a small group, who sat on mats. Autry could see another bunch of kids on playground equipment in the backyard, and in a sit-ting area, two teachers held babies. Clearly, business was good at Just Us Kids.

"Autry, welcome!" his sister-in-law Bella said, get-ting up from the reception desk. Though she was the manager of the center, she often filled in when someone else was out for the day. "I'll lead the way to Walker's office. He's waiting for you."

Autry smiled at Bella and followed her to a small room in the back. Walker sat behind a desk, going over papers in a folder. He nodded at his brother. "Hudson's got a bad cold, so I'm handling business here today and tomorrow. Got the paperwork?"

Autry was getting used to seeing Walker in this en-vironment, his usual Italian suits replaced by more ca-sual clothes. Plus, the man had different-colored paint splotches on the back of his hands, which suggested he'd joined a few toddlers at their painting session.

Autry handed him the folder. "All signed and ready to go."

"Flight leaves day after tomorrow, right?" Walker asked.

"Yup. At 6:30 p.m. I have to admit, I'm going to miss this place. Rust Creek Falls, I mean."

Walker glanced up from the sheaf of papers. "So stay. Move here. Hudson says you're hot and heavy with Marissa Fuller. You going to walk away from her?"

Stab to the heart. "Yeah, I am. I care about her, but my life is a jet plane, Walker. I like it here, yes. I like Marissa. But I also like global travel. I like my job. I like negotiating deals for Jones Holdings. I like the history of the family business, the generations of Joneses behind it. I'm invested in the company's future. That means leaving."

Walker leaned back in his chair and observed his younger brother. "Huh. Guess the water or the punch didn't work its magic on you. Dad's influence is too strong."

Autry pictured his father sitting in his leather desk chair, imperious and impervious, his life about business and mergers and acquisitions. He wasn't like his dad. He knew people mattered more than business. But another difference between his father and Autry was that Autry hadn't made any promises to anyone in the form of vows or fatherhood to be there, to be present. He'd been straight up with Marissa from the get-go. No commitment. And she'd been the same. No strings. They'd had a good time. A magical time. But now that time had come to the end they always knew was waiting.

"It's not about Dad. It's about who I am. I like this town more than I ever thought I would. But I can't see myself settled down here, Walker."

"Maybe because leaving every couple of months is easier than building a life somewhere."

Autry shrugged. "Okay, Dr. Phil."

Walker laughed. "It's been great having you here, Autry. I hope you'll come visit in between countries."

"I definitely will," he said.

Walker stood up and the brothers embraced, and then Autry headed back out, stopping to smile at a little boy making faces at him through the sliding glass door to the backyard. Autry waved at the kid, who seemed disappointed that he wasn't getting chastised by the grown-up. Just then another boy called to him, and the two scamps went to play on a slide. Autry watched them giggle their way back up the ladder a second time, sending pebbles down the slide and chasing after them. Autry smiled; he could remember doing that with his brothers when they were kids. He could watch this kind of thing all day.

Wait. What? He could? The last time he'd been here, his collar had tightened on him to the point he was at risk of being strangled by his own three-hundred-dollar shirt. Now he was buoyed by the sight of an impish kid and a buddy racing around? *Eh, maybe it was a good sign.* That time really did heal all wounds. Spending these weeks with the Fuller girls had helped him overcome that old ache of seeing babies and toddlers and children, which had been a constant reminder of what he'd lost—little Lulu and who she'd become as she grew up.

Okay, so he could now walk into a day care without feeling the need to race out and find a kid-free zone. That didn't mean he was anywhere close to being a family kind of guy. Or else he wouldn't have been so torn up by what Abby had said last night.

Thanks for making me remember what it's like to have a dad. It sure is nice.

That old ache gripped him by the chest and squeezed. Autry frowned and slid on his sunglasses and left.

So much for change.

His cell phone rang—Marissa's home phone number.

"Autry, it's Roberta Rafferty."

"Roberta, this is a nice surprise. What can I do for you?"

"You could come to a going-away party for yourself tomorrow at five thirty. Ralph is doing the grilling this time. Your responsibility is just to have a good time and a wonderful send-off."

He didn't think he could take a whole evening with Marissa, knowing she'd be out of his life the next day, without imploding. "Roberta, that's very kind of you, but not nec—"

"After everything you did for my family these past few weeks, oh yes, it is necessary. I won't hear another word. We will see you at five thirty tomorrow. Don't bring a thing but yourself."

"Well, I can't promise I won't bring anything, but I'll be there."

"Good. See you then."

That was interesting, Autry thought, as he pocketed his phone. He hadn't thought Roberta was part of his fan club. Now she was throwing a party in his honor.

One thing was for sure when it came to the Fuller-Raffertys. He never knew what to expect.

* * *

As Marissa watched her daughters stack paper plates and plastic cups on the buffet table for Autry's bon-voyage party, she could swear that Kaylee was taller by at least an inch and that Kiera's hair had gotten very long over the summer and that Abby, who was teaching herself Spanish via a website so that she could learn 2LOVEU songs in two languages, was growing up way too fast. School was starting next week, and both Kaylee and Kiera were having firsts. Kaylee would start preschool and Kiera would start kindergarten.

And now that her younger girls would be in school a good chunk of the day, Marissa was going to talk to her boss about increasing her hours back to full-time. This way she could help her parents more financially and save up to send them on the Caribbean cruise they'd always wanted.

Maybe Marissa would even adopt one of Helen's little pups when the three available were ready. Abby had always wanted a dog, but Marissa hadn't been sure she could handle one more thing to take care of, and Roberta didn't love pet hair on her clothes. Anyway, it was just something to think about for the future.

She was thinking about anything and everything to avoid what was constantly trying to push its way into the forefront of her mind: Autry. When her mother had told her that the Raffertys were throwing a good-bye party for him, Marissa had been shocked—then not so shocked. Her mother had fallen under Autry's spell. It was hard not to. He was a great man. Kind, generous, warm.

And so damned sexy and great in bed that Marissa

could still feel every imprint on her body where his hands and lips had been.

She was glad they'd had sex. It wasn't a mistake and there were no regrets. She'd needed that night and she'd wanted him, and she'd taken what was being offered: one amazing night that she'd never forget and that would sustain her probably for years given just how earthmoving it had been. She smiled, but felt the smile fading. She would never feel his hands on her again after the perfunctory goodbye hug he'd give her after the party. She'd never feel his lips on hers. Maybe every couple years he'd come to town to visit his brothers and he'd stop by to say hello.

She wrapped her arms around her middle as a sadness crept inside her heart.

Then she lifted her chin and pasted a smile on her face. For the sake of her girls, especially for Abby, she'd act like everything was fine, that of course she'd miss Autry, but they always knew he was leaving, et cetera, et cetera. She'd put on a happy expression for the girls, then disappear into the bathroom or her room to cry if she felt tears coming. And she had no doubt they would.

At five thirty, her father had just put the burgers, marinated chicken and steaks on the grill with some veggie kebabs and corn on the cob in the husk, when Autry came around the yard, carrying two big shopping bags.

"I ordered that man not to bring anything," Roberta whispered in Marissa's ear.

Marissa smiled and felt the smile wobble, so she corrected it. Her girls were just a few feet away and watching her. How did Autry manage to look more handsome every time she saw him? He wore a dark blue Henley shirt and jeans and his AJ belt buckle.

"Mom! Mr. Autry is here!" Abby shrieked and raced over to him for a hug.

He bent over to wrap Abby in his arms, then scooped up the younger girls and swung them around. "Hey, Fuller girls," he said.

"What's in the bags?" Kaylee asked, peering in.

"Kaylee, that's not polite!" Abby chastised, also trying to peer inside. Marissa always appreciated when Abby did her work for her.

"Well, I might have a going-away present for my favorite three kids," Autry said with a grin.

Roberta leaned close to Marissa and whispered, "He's generous to a fault!"

"He's thoughtful," Marissa whispered back.

Her mom nodded. "That, too."

Kiera tilted her head, her long brown ponytail falling over one shoulder. "But you're the one going away, not us."

"Yeah. That's why *we* made *you* going-away presents," Abby said.

"What? Presents for me?" Autry touched his heart. "That's real nice of you, girls."

Kiera and Kaylee ran over to the table where they'd been working on the gifts and wrapping them this afternoon.

"Kaylee, you first," Abby said, like a little mother. "Then Kiera, then me."

Kaylee grinned and held out the gift she'd wrapped herself. The bright red sparkly paper didn't quite reach the back. Marissa held in a smile. Autry sat on the grass and gently opened it on his lap.

Marissa watched Autry closely; the man was clearly touched by the paper plate that Kaylee had decorated with feathers and glitter and wrote inside a big heart: Mr. Autry Is Nice.

"I love this," he said, giving her a big hug. "Thank you, Kaylee."

Next up was Kiera. Autry opened her gift, and for a second, Marissa wondered if he didn't like it. It was a photograph of him and the three Fuller girls that Ralph had taken during the last few weeks. They were in the backyard, under a tree, a soccer ball in Kiera's arms. She'd made the frame herself at an arts-and-crafts camp this summer.

"I'll treasure this," he said. "Thank you, Kiera."

Kiera beamed. "This way you won't forget us. When you go away."

He hugged her again. "I'd never forget you guys. Impossible."

"And now it's my turn," Abby said. "My present isn't something you can wrap. It's a song I'm going to sing."

Marissa watched her daughter bite her lip and stand back, as though the nine-year-old wasn't sure Autry would like her gift. Though Marissa had helped the younger girls make and wrap their presents, Abby wanted to do hers on her own. She'd spent the afternoon in her room working on it, so Marissa had no clue what the song was. But a song seemed a lovely idea for a send-off.

Abby walked over to the patio table bench and turned on her iPod and the speaker, and the tune of 2LOVEU's megahit "Only You" filled the air, but just the music, not the lyrics.

Abby cleared her throat. "I made up new lyrics to the song. Okay, here it goes."

Everyone quieted and sat down, excited to hear Abby's song.

"Oh, Mr. Autry, oh, oh, oh, at first you were just our mom's new friend," Abby sang, "but then you became our friend, too-oo-oo."

Kiera and Kaylee clapped, shaking their little bodies to the music.

Marissa glanced at Autry. He was smiling and she could tell he was deeply touched.

"You made us steaks and played charades..." Abby sang, "and even when you lost, you always smiled." The audience laughed and then the chorus swelled; Abby held her fist to her mouth as though it were a microphone. "And then you stepped in as my partner for the kids competition... Yeah, and I realized that only you could be our new dad. Ooh, yeah," she sang. "Only you-oo-oo. Only you."

Marissa froze and watched as Autry's face paled. She glanced at her parents. Her mother's expression was tight; her dad tapping his foot to the music as though he hadn't fully registered what Abby had just sung.

"Yeah, ooh, yeah, only you," Abby finished and took a bow.

Everyone clapped and Marissa watched Autry try to recover. Abby ran over to give him a hug and he hugged her tight.

"That was really nice," he said. "You have a great voice."

She waited for him to say more. Marissa recognized the look in her daughter's eyes from when Abby would

ask Marissa for something, be told no and then wait
for a change of mind.

Autry said nothing else.

Abby's smile was tight like Roberta's.

Oh God. Exactly what they'd been afraid of happening had happened.

Ralph announced that dinner was ready, and Marissa was grateful for the distraction. The crew headed
over to the buffet table and filled their plates, then sat
down. Ralph asked Autry all kinds of questions about
Paris, and as Autry described all the exciting sights,
like the Louvre and the famous *Mona Lisa* painting and
the breathtaking Eiffel Tower, the Fuller girls, including even subdued Abby, were transfixed. Autry, who
was just about fluent in four languages, spoke French
to the girls, and they were delighted to hear that "I
love hamburgers with pickles and mustard" sounded
so fancy in that language.

Every now and again, Marissa would catch Autry
looking at her, and she tried to keep her expression
neutral and the conversation focused on his trip—not
how she felt. Which was absolutely miserable.

She loved Autry. She loved him with all her heart.
And tomorrow he was flying off to Paris.

After dessert of ice cream and fruit, her parents insisted on cleaning up themselves, no help allowed. Abby
got a phone call from her friend Janie and disappeared
with Marissa's phone into her bedroom. Marissa, Autry
and the two younger girls played charades, Kiera standing up and holding up three fingers to indicate that her
charade was three words. But then she glanced back
toward the house. "Hey, wait. Where's Abby? I can't do

this one if she's not here. It's 2LOVEU." She plastered her hand over her mouth. "Oops! I just gave it away."

Yeah, where is Abby? Marissa thought. She'd gone into the house with the phone at least fifteen minutes ago. Granted, the girl loved to talk on the phone to Janie, but it was unusual for her to stay away this long when Autry was over.

Marissa's parents came back out just then, and Marissa asked them to stay with the girls while she went to get Abby.

As she headed into the house, she realized Autry was right behind her.

"I think I should handle this," she said. "It's my fault." Tears poked her eyes but she blinked them back.

"Your fault? How? What do you mean?"

"I have a feeling that Abby is in her room upset about the reaction to the song. The lack of reaction, I should say, from you. I don't mean that you should have jumped up and said, 'Yes, I'd love to be your daddy.' Of course not. But…" She stopped, her heart clenching.

"But what?" he said flatly.

"My mother tried to warn me that Abby was the one who'd get hurt. But I let this happen, anyway. I let you come into our lives. I let you do The Great Roundup Kids Competition with her. I let you take us all on that dream trip to the 2LOVEU concert. I let her love you."

The tears she'd fought did come then and Marissa wiped them away. *I let myself love you.*

What had she done? Why wasn't she more protective of her children? Of herself?

Autry put his hands on her shoulders. "Marissa, I'm here now. And I'd like to try to fix this—somehow. Let me at least try to talk to her."

She sucked in a deep breath, torn in two. "Okay."

They headed up the stairs together, both silent.

Marissa knocked on Abby's door, then opened it. The room was empty. "That's weird. She's not here and we didn't pass her in the living room."

"She couldn't have gotten far," Autry said. "Let's split up and check the house and property."

"It's a big property. Over five acres. The girls don't go into the wooded area unless they're with us, and besides, we would have seen Abby come outside and head toward the woods. Where can she be?"

"We'll find her. I promise you."

Marissa's heart turned over. Where was her daughter?

Chapter Fifteen

While Marissa checked the house, Autry went to the front yard to see if Abby had gone outside. He glanced around at the big lawn, the huge trees dotting the property. In between the heavy green leaf cover of one, he could just make out a pair of orange sneakers with bright yellow laces dangling from blue-jeaned legs. Abby had climbed a tree and was sitting on a branch, not that high up, but higher than his eye level.

Be careful, he told himself as he walked over. He had no idea what he was going to say. He just knew whatever did come out of his mouth would come from his heart and would be the truth, whatever that was. The truth always did out.

"Hey," he called up, leaning against the trunk of the tree.

He noticed Marissa looking out the window from the living room and caught her eye; he gestured toward the branch and gave her a thumbs-up, then pointed to himself to let her know he had this. She nodded and stayed put, moving a bit out of view.

"Abby?"

He heard her crying, which turned into full sobs.

"Janie called to tell me that Lyle is leaving the band. Leaving 2LOVEU. Can you believe that? He's the lead singer! And my favorite." A fresh round of sobs ensued.

"I'm sorry to hear that, Abby. I know how much you like him. But, sweetie, why'd you come out here all by yourself? If you'd told your mom why you were upset, she could have made things better."

"No, she couldn't have!" Abby blurted out, anger lacing her voice. "Mom wouldn't understand at all. Mom is so strong and doesn't need anybody, but I do!"

Oh, Abby, he thought, his heart going out to the girl. "Sweets, everyone needs people. Everyone."

"Nope," she insisted. "I miss my daddy all the time, but Mom barely talks about him. And now you're leaving, too, and Mom is acting like she doesn't even care." She broke into more sobs. "Everyone always leaves. Everyone!"

Autry climbed up next to Abby, praying the branch would hold his weight. It seemed steady. He pulled Abby into his arms and let her cry it out, leaning his head on top of hers.

"I might be leaving tomorrow," Autry said, "but I will always be there for you, Abby. If you need me, text me. Call me. I'm a friend of the Fuller-Rafferty family, Abby, and that's what close friends do—they're there for each other."

"I can text you?" she asked. "If I want to tell you something?"

"You bet," he said. "Even if it's a bad joke. Or if you bomb a spelling test."

She laughed. "I'm a really good speller."

"Then text me about an A-plus on your spelling test. Bad news. Good news. That's what people who care about you are for. And I care, Abby. Even if I'm thousands of miles away. An ocean away."

"Too bad Lyle doesn't care," she said, rolling her eyes.

"You know celebs," he said. "But you know, you can still love listening to their music even if Lyle's leaving. There's always going to be change in your life, Abby. And you yourself will change constantly, too. That's what growing up is all about."

"My mom says growing up is full of ups and downs, but more ups."

"Your mom is one smart cookie. Life is amazing. I've had some downs, but look—here I am, hanging out with one of my favorite people in a tree. Pretty cool, huh?"

She laughed. "Yeah. It is."

"Should we go join the party? I hear your grand-father is making those lime rickeys I love so much."

Her face brightened and she wrapped her arms around him. "Thanks, Mr. Autry."

"Anytime," he said and kissed the top of her head.

As if he were her father. Or something like it.

Relief had flooded Marissa when Autry had indi-cated that he'd found Abby. Then anger. At herself. For letting him into their lives.

If it had been just her, just her heart that would be shredded when he left, fine. But she'd let her children experience the whirlwind magic of Autry Jones, and now her child was crying in a tree.

And hadn't come to her.

Marissa froze when the realization struck. Abby hadn't come to her. Why?

She peered out the window and saw Abby and Autry heading back toward the house, Autry's arm around her, Abby animatedly talking about something. Well, whatever he'd said had been the right thing.

They came in the front door, and her daughter ran into her arms.

"I'm sorry I just left, Mom. I was so upset because Janie called and told me that Lyle is leaving 2LOVEU. And that combined with Autry leaving... I just kinda lost it."

Marissa hugged her daughter. "I understand, sweetie. But next time you're sad about something, I hope you'll come to me, Abby. You can always tell me anything."

"Mr. Autry says you're a smart cookie. I already know that." Abby hugged her tight. "I'm going to help Grandpa make the lime rickeys. Mr. Autry loves those." She ran off toward the kitchen.

Marissa turned to Autry. "Thanks for talking to her. Whatever you said was obviously the right thing."

"I just let her know that I care about her and I'm here for her, even if I'm three thousand miles away. That if she needs a friend she can always text me."

Ah. Well, that was nice of him. Marissa wasn't sure how long that would last. Maybe the first couple weeks, he'd be charmed by a nine-year-old texting him that she was upset about a boy teasing her or something. But then he'd stop being so charmed and would take longer and longer to respond, until he stopped altogether. And then Marissa would have to deal with Abby's tears over that. So why prolong the inevitable?

"Marissa, I…"

And he still hadn't said anything about Abby's song. About how only Autry could be their new dad. He was ignoring, avoiding it. Because he couldn't be their dad. Wouldn't be. Didn't want to be.

And, hell, was Marissa ready for someone to step into their lives just like that?

Whatever. He wasn't asking to stay, anyway. He wasn't asking to be her children's father.

"I care about all of you, Marissa. You know that. I wish things could be different."

Right. If wishes…

She lifted her chin, ignoring the stabbing sensation in her chest. "After the lime rickeys, I think you should go, Autry. Give everyone a hug goodbye and then…go. Tomorrow, just leave. No stopping over, no calls. Tonight is it."

He sucked in a breath and ran his hand through that sexy dark blond hair. "Marissa—"

"There's nothing to say, Autry. I thank you from the bottom of my heart for a magical three weeks. But even if you were the small-town type, which you aren't and never will be, who says *I'm* ready for a relationship? I wasn't ready to date when you sauntered into town. I'm still not. There's just too much to consider and too much on my plate, like my daughters' lives and hearts. So these weeks were all we'd ever have, anyway."

For a moment before he walked away, he'd held her gaze, and she wished she were a mind reader. She knew he didn't love her. Maybe if he did he'd fight for them.

But what was there to fight for? He was leaving. To-morrow.

"Mommy! Mr. Autry is handing out presents!" Kiera called.

She closed her eyes, grateful for the privacy of the foyer. Bracing herself, she forced herself into the back-yard. Abby was modeling her new school backpack, her initials embroidered across the pocket in hot pink. Inside were school supplies, everything she needed, which meant he'd actually gone on her school website and looked up the list for the fourth grade. He'd even managed to find a 2LOVEU pencil case.

"Lyle might be leaving 2LOVEU but that doesn't mean I can't still love their music," she said. "And I got to see them before they broke up!"

Kiera had a new backpack, too, her very first, with her initials embroidered in her favorite color, royal blue. Inside was a monkey key ring holder to chain on the outside loop and school supplies for the kin-dergarten class.

And Kaylee, starting preschool, had brand-new light-up sneakers in her favorite color, purple. She was jumping around the yard, showing them off.

The Raffertys received a voucher for a cruise around the Caribbean islands anytime in the next year. Ralph was still gasping, and Roberta had tears in her eyes.

"You all have given me so much, you have no idea," Autry said. "I came to Rust Creek Falls a different per-son. I'm leaving a changed man. Thank you."

The three Fuller girls fell on him, crying and hug-ging and laughing.

And then Marissa walked Autry to the door.

"Last but not least," he said, handing her a small wrapped box.

"I don't think I should," she said.

He tilted up her chin with his finger. "Please."

She took the gift and unwrapped it. It was a light blue box she'd recognize anywhere. She opened the lid. Inside was a heart-shaped locket. She opened the locket and there was a tiny photo of her and her three girls. On the back was engraved: *You changed my life. AJ.*

Don't cry, don't cry, don't cry, she told herself.

"Thank you, Autry."

He took the box and set it on the hall table, then fastened the locket around her neck. Then he took her face in his hands and kissed her. One more time.

One last time.

And then he was gone.

Passport, check. Boarding pass stored electronically, check. Tablet, phone, Thorpe Corp. folder for the flight, check.

Autry checked and rechecked his carry-on bag in his room at Maverick Manor, anything to avoid thinking about the house he'd left a little while ago. The family he'd said goodbye to.

He wasn't a small-town guy—that was true. And he'd never be. That was true, too. But he was a Fuller-Rafferty guy. His brothers had found happiness settling down here, so why did the idea of it fill Autry with a sense of dread?

Because it's not right for you. No matter how much you love Marissa.

He did love her.

And he loved her kids.

But he knew where that led, and maybe that was why he couldn't imagine settling down here. Maybe it wasn't so much that he wasn't a small-town guy as he wasn't a settling down guy. He wasn't a family guy. He might have become pretty good at soothing tears and choosing gifts and playing charades, but that didn't mean the life was for him.

You loved and you got stomped on. That's what he knew for sure. That had been the case in his life ever since he was a kid. His father had disappointed him time and again. His mother had forgotten his and his brothers' birthdays several times as they'd grown up. Maybe with five kids that happened.

Autry doubted that. If Marissa had ten kids, she'd know their birthdays.

But then he'd finally let love in and Karinna had taken a bat to his heart. He'd lost her and Lulu. And now he'd let in Marissa and her three girls. Hell, he'd let in her parents. And someday, Marissa would probably realize that he'd been her rebound guy, her entrée to dating, and she'd find the guy she really loved, the guy she was supposed to be with. Not some jet-setter whose life she didn't understand.

He thought of his father, and how he'd failed to bring Walker Jones the Second closer to Walker the Third and Hudson. He'd had three weeks, and all his attempts to make his father see reason, see love when it was right in front of him in the form of his happy sons, had been fruitless.

He was giving it one more try.

He pulled out his phone and pressed in his dad's number.

"Ah, good, Autry," his father said. "Did you convince those brothers of yours to see reason and move home?"

Autry shook his head, literally and figuratively. "With or without their wives?"

"With, of course. Once they see Tulsa, both women will never want to go back to that dot on the map. Is Rust Falls Creek even on the map?"

"*Rust Creek Falls*, Dad. And doesn't it mean anything to you to know that Walker and Hudson are happy? Truly happy?"

"Of course. But I don't see why they can't be happy in Tulsa."

"Is that Autry, dear?" he heard his mother say. "Let me talk to him."

"Autry, honey, I hope you'll be a better influence on Gideon and Jensen than Walker and Hudson have been on you and your younger brothers. You are leaving for Paris tomorrow, right?"

Autry could only hope his two younger brothers were as lucky as Walker and Hudson some day. "I am leaving tomorrow. But Mom, you and Dad are being unfair to Walker and Hudson—and their wives. They're happy. Truly happy. I wish you could understand that."

"We do, dear. It's difficult to understand how they could be happy in that town, but if they are, they are."

That was the best he was going to get. Resignation and acceptance. Unbelievable.

"Well, your father and I are off to a fund-raiser. Best to your brothers. Bye, dear."

He'd tried.

When he thought of the differences between his

family and the Fuller-Raffertys, it was almost comical. Polar opposites.

He sat on the edge of his bed and pulled out the antique pocket watch he'd bought in the Rust Creek Falls thrift shop. Twenty bucks and he loved it. The minute he'd seen the old bronze cover with a compass symbol on the front, he'd known he had to have it. And he'd printed out another copy of the photo he'd put in Marissa's locket and put it on the left side of the pocket watch.

He clicked it open now and there they were. Marissa and her daughters.

The family he was walking away from.

His heart heavy, he closed the watch and put it in his carry-on, then went out to say a final goodbye to the town, the general store and the doughnut shop and the Ace in the Hole. He wanted to stop by all the places he'd visited while in town. And then tomorrow night, he'd be on a plane, headed toward the future.

For a moment he let himself imagine staying here. Moving here. Shipping the contents of his office to the Jones Holdings, Inc. in Rust Creek Falls. He and Walker would probably order in from the Ace all the time. He smiled at the thought.

Except he didn't want to move to Rust Creek Falls. He didn't want to work out of this town. He wanted to go to Paris. He'd be there for at least a year.

And all he'd have to remind him of Marissa? Her picture in a pocket watch.

He'd said goodbye. She'd said goodbye. And reminded him that she wasn't up for a relationship, anyway. Not a real one. Three weeks when she knew he was leaving—that was one thing for a widow with a lot on her plate and three young lives to manage. A real, in-person, constant relationship with a man was something else. She hadn't been planning on that.

So that was that.

His heart breaking, Autry headed out to say goodbye to this town that had slipped inside his heart when he wasn't looking.

Chapter Sixteen

Autry woke up at the crack of dawn. The sun was just peeking over the horizon. He'd barely slept, his hand wrapped around his phone, the need to call Marissa and hear her voice so strong it took everything in him not to press in her number. Last night, when he'd walked around Rust Creek Falls, saying his mental goodbye to this special town, everything had reminded him of her and the girls. He'd been about to swing by the Ace in the Hole and have a draft when a pang hit him so hard he'd avoided Sawmill Street entirely. He would never forget looking around the crowded bar and the entire world falling away except for that brunette beauty's lovely face, the twinkle in her dark eyes, the way her silky brown hair fell over her shoulders. A single mother in a T-shirt and shorts, though of course he hadn't known she was a single mother then.

I didn't know you were a single mother... I wouldn't have approached you...

He remembered the look on her face when he'd said those cruel words. At the time he'd thought the truth was all that mattered, and, yeah, the truth always mattered. But he didn't have to say that. You couldn't fix some things to make other things work, but nothing would change the fact that Marissa Fuller was a single mom.

Except if you married her, he could hear his brother Hudson saying as a joke, with a Groucho Marx wiggle of his eyebrows.

A new truth? Autry could see himself married to Marissa. He could see himself as a father to her daughters, the three girls he'd come to love despite all his trying not to. He smiled, thinking about how easy it was for the Fuller family to get inside his heart. Just by existing. By being themselves.

But then there was another truth—that Marissa lived here in Rust Creek Falls and he was about to leave for Paris for a year. He was going to Paris; there was no getting around that, and he didn't want to get around it. This trip was important to him, to the family business. And Marissa and her daughters were important. But they lived here.

Problem.

Autry pulled a fluffy down pillow over his head and groaned. He chucked the pillow aside and got out of bed and took a hot shower. Under the spray of the water he realized that maybe he should go say goodbye to the Ace in the Hole. Maybe doing so would give him some closure. He'd see the place where it had all started, acknowledge it and accept that this was just how it was, and then he'd board his corporate jet for France.

It was barely six o'clock in the morning and the Ace

wasn't open, but he figured he could just peer in the windows. Except as he approached, there was a light on inside, a dim light over by the pool table. A sign on the door said the bar's hours were noon to 1:30 a.m., so the place definitely wasn't open. But he could see two people inside, talking and hugging and sipping something from mugs. Maybe they wouldn't mind if he came in and just took one last look around?

He tried the door and it opened. The couple, a man and a woman, started, clearly not expecting anyone to be coming into the bar at 6:00 a.m.

"Sorry to barge in on your—" he began to say, then froze.

Whoa. He was pretty darn sure that Brenna O'Reilly and Travis Dalton, of *The Great Roundup* fame, stood not two feet in front of him. He'd seen them around town over the past few weeks but hadn't had an opportunity to meet either of them since both were always surrounded by friends and family and fans. Brenna's long red hair was up in a bun or something and hidden under a hot-pink cowboy hat, and Travis wore his dark brown Stetson low over his forehead, but the dark hair, bright blue eyes and confident expression was unmistakable. He had no idea why they were here at the crack of dawn but that was none of his business.

"—private something or other," Autry finished. "I just wanted to take a look around for old times' sake."

"Old times' sake?" Travis said. "Look, I'd know a Jones brother anywhere, and you are definitely a Jones. You have the face and the four-hundred-dollar shoes. But how could there be an old times' sake for you here in Rust Creek Falls? Aren't you from Oklahoma?"

He laughed and extended his right hand. "Autry

Jones. I've been here for a few weeks visiting Hudson and Walker. And I met someone here, someone pretty special."

"Ah. Love. Got me, too," Travis said, grabbing Brenna around the waist and pulling her close.

"Yup, a Jones, all right," Brenna said, studying him as she shimmied out of Travis's hold. "I'm Brenna Dal—O'Reilly," she added fast. "And this is my—this is my fiancé, Travis Dalton."

"The two of you need no introductions," Autry said. "I've now seen three episodes of *The Great Roundup*. Great job on that button-sewing challenge, Brenna."

Brenna beamed. "Thanks. So this special person you met here. Why isn't she with you?"

Autry sighed. "I'm leaving the country on business today. For a year. And Marissa lives here."

"Marissa? Marissa Fuller?" Brenna asked. "We went to high school together—well, I was a year behind her. I always looked up to Marissa. She knew what she wanted and nothing stood in her way, you know? She had a life plan. I was more a wild child—until this guy made it easy to settle down. Okay, fine, I've loved Travis Dalton since I was a kid."

A life plan. Marissa's life plan had gotten a left hook to it. That was how it was, though. Who was it who said that life happened when you were making other plans?

Autry smiled. "You two are lucky."

"You could be, too, man," Travis said. "If you want this woman, go get her. That's all there is to it. If you can walk away, then do that. That's how you'll know. You're either going to break down her door—though I wouldn't recommend that, since I know Marissa and her kids live with her parents, and you don't mess with

Roberta Rafferty—or you're going to catch a plane to wherever. So which is it gonna be? You don't have to answer that now."

Good, because Autry didn't have an answer.

"I'm sorry I barged in," he said. "Looks like you two are having a little private remembrance of your own."

"No problem," Travis said. "We sneaked in for some time alone in one of our favorite places. Since the show's aired, we get mobbed. If we want to make out and slow dance, we have to do it at 6:00 a.m. in a closed bar."

Brenna laughed. "I like all the attention, though. Filming on location was exciting, but there's no place like home, and Rust Creek Falls is home. I used to think I couldn't wait to leave this small town, but I was sure wrong."

"Thanks to me," Travis said, swooping her into his arms. "You would never have left town or Bee's Beauty Salon with me still here, and you know it."

"Darn tooting I wouldn't have," Brenna said, winking. "And now you're mine."

They started making out, so that was Autry's cue to leave. He took one last look around, his gaze stopping on the table where Marissa had sat with her friend Anne. His heart had stopped in that moment he'd first seen Marissa. And restarted—without him realizing just how restarted it was.

You're either going to break down her door...or you're going to catch a plane...

The problem was, he wanted to do both.

Marissa glanced at the alarm clock on her bedside table. It was 6:20 a.m. and she hadn't slept a wink.

She'd tossed and turned, Autry Jones's face flashing in her mind all night long like a blinking neon sign. She'd heard his voice, seen him hugging her girls, talking for hours with her dad about stocks and fishing. And then she remembered their night in Seattle in his hotel room, where they'd finally made love.

Would that be enough? One amazing night with Autry to remember him by?

It wasn't like she had a choice. She had to let him go.

She reached into the bookshelf below her bedside table and pulled out one of the photo albums she kept there. Sometimes, when the girls couldn't sleep and would come tearfully into her room, talking about monsters and bad dreams and sore gums, she'd lie with one or two or all three Fuller girls and pull out the album and show them pictures of themselves as babies, their father holding them. And they'd quiet down like magic, loving to look at their dad and see what they couldn't remember. Abby could, of course; she'd been seven when they lost Mike Fuller, and one of the last things he did was teach her to ride a two-wheeler. Marissa had photographic evidence of her wipeouts, of Mike holding the back of the bike as she pedaled along, of Abby soaring down the sidewalk, Mike pumping his fist in the air. Abby loved that photo.

On the first page of the album were pictures from high school, Marissa and Mike holding hands, kissing under the bleachers on the baseball field. And of prom night, when Abby was conceived. Then there were the wedding pictures, the reception in the Raffertys' backyard and the tiny first house they'd rented in town, new parents at eighteen.

This is your life, Marissa Fuller, she thought, flipping the pages, smiling, a tear coming, her heart comforted. *This was your life. But you'll always have your memories and Mike will always live on in your daughters.*

She was saying goodbye, she realized. To who she used to be. And she was ready to be this new person. Not a woman in transition. But a new Marissa.

Autry had helped her become that new person. And for that, she would love him forever. Even though she'd have to do it from thousands of miles away.

"Mr. Autry is so lucky," Kiera said as Marissa put two "face" pancakes on each girl's plate. She'd made eyes with blueberries and a smiling mouth with cut-up strawberries.

Marissa eyed the clock on the wall. It was 8:30 a.m. She was exhausted from not sleeping and from getting up so early, but she felt like the new person she'd claimed to be. Today was the first day of the rest of her life. She wasn't going to mope about Autry. She was going to be this new Marissa, one who'd loved and lost—twice—but who relished memories and learned from her mistakes and kept putting one foot in front of the other. Her heart was open. That was the key. She was ready to accept new people. New experiences. New ideas. That was the kind of mother she wanted to be for her girls. Someone who took risks—well, the right risks. Falling for Autry had been the right risk. Yes, she was losing him today. But he'd been worth it. Everything about these three weeks had been worth it.

"Why is Mr. Autry lucky?" Kaylee asked, taking a strip of bacon from the platter in the center of the table.

Abby poured maple syrup on her pancakes. "Yeah, why?"

"Because he's gonna live where the little cute rats are the cooks," Kiera said. "Paris is where Remy lives, right? I would love if a funny rat in a chef hat made my pancakes."

"What?" Marissa asked. Rats? Working in restaurants? And who was Remy?

Thank heavens her parents had gone out to breakfast with their friends. Her mother did not like rats. And Ralph would get the broom out at the very mention.

Abby laughed. "We woke up kinda early this morning and I was saying I was gonna miss Autry and suggested we watch the movie *Ratatouille* because it takes place in Paris—where Autry is going."

Marissa raised an eyebrow. "Ratatouille? Isn't that a vegetable stew?"

Kiera laughed. "Mommy! The rat is the cook who makes stew. And other yummy stuff."

Abby nodded. "Mom, don't you remember the movie? Remy's the rat who wanted to be a real chef, so he started helping out the restaurant worker guy who couldn't cook? The guy got all the credit, but Remy was happy just cooking."

Marissa shivered. "I vaguely remember. Rats, even cartoon rats, freak me out a little. I don't think I'd want a rat making my dinner."

"But Remy was so cute!" Kaylee said.

Kiera nodded. "I wish I could have a pet rat."

Oh no. Not happening.

"I'll bet the most amazing things happen in Paris," Abby said, her eyes all dreamy. "Thinking about Paris helps me not think about Lyle. I still don't know how he could leave 2LOVEU. But Autry was right. Change is part of life."

Change was definitely a part of life, Marissa thought, Autry's handsome face coming to mind. She wondered what he was doing. Packing, probably. Having his last breakfast in Rust Creek Falls with his brothers and their wives.

"We've been through lots of changes," Kiera said, popping a blueberry in her mouth.

Kaylee looked at her big sisters. "I have a change. I want to change to eating bacon now."

Abby laughed and passed her little sister a strip of bacon.

"Maybe we could learn French," Abby said. "Mom, I was studying Spanish so I could learn 2LOVEU songs in two languages, but now I want to switch to French. I wonder how you say hello in French."

"I think it's *bonjour*," Marissa said, slugging down her coffee. "I think it translates to *good day*." The last thing she wanted to talk about was Paris. And Autry. But the girls needed to and so she would.

"How do you say goodbye?" Kiera asked.

"I'm pretty sure it's *adieu* or *au revoir*," Marissa said, her appetite waning.

"We had to say adieu to Autry," Kiera said. "I miss him already. I wish he could have breakfast with us." She frowned and put down her fork.

"Me, too," Kaylee said. "He's nice. I love my new backpack."

"Me, three," Abby said. "It doesn't feel right not to say goodbye the day he's leaving."

Three girls turned their gazes on Marissa.

Au revoir. Adieu. Goodbye. They'd said their good-byes yesterday.

And today was the first day of the rest of her life. Wasn't that what she'd said for the past two hours? She was a new person thanks to Autry, and she would start being that new person by letting him go. Because she didn't have a choice.

Right. She had no choice. He was leaving. But…

But she could tell the man how she felt about him. *You told him you weren't ready for a relationship. But you're ready for him. Autry Jones. The man you love.*

Tell him. Just tell him. He'll go to Paris and you'll be here, but at least you'll have said it. The new Marissa said what was on her mind. And in her heart. She didn't hide her feelings. She didn't pretend she had no feelings.

As the girls realized she wasn't answering, they went back to eating their breakfast, if a little more glumly than a minute ago.

Phone in hand, she went into the living room for a little privacy. She tried Autry's room at Maverick Manor, but was told he'd checked out a half hour ago.

No. No, no, no. She'd missed him? She tried his cell phone, but it went straight to voice mail.

He wasn't leaving Rust Creek Falls without knowing how she felt. That she loved him. That he'd opened her eyes, opened her heart. She loved him and she'd scream it from the rooftop of the Ace in the Hole if she had to.

So do it. Go scream it.

An idea started forming in her head. Could she? Would she?

"Girls, put on your sneakers."

"Why? Where are we going?"

No, they weren't headed for the Ace in the Hole so she could climb up onto the roof and shout "I love Autry Jones!" for all the town to hear. Though she was so crazy in love she just might, if it came to that.

"Where are we going?" she repeated. "To the airport, even though it's a very long drive. We have a man to say goodbye to." The airport was three hours away, but it would be worth every mile.

"Yay!" Abby shouted. "Oh, Mom, I knew yesterday couldn't have been our final chance to say goodbye. Not when we have this morning."

What was that famous movie line? From *Casablanca*. "We'll always have Paris." She and Autry wouldn't, but yes, they'd have this morning. In the airport. Though by the time they got there, it would be afternoon. Closer and closer to his six-thirty departure.

Kiera and Kaylee raced to the hall closet and stuffed their feet into their sneakers, Kaylee wearing her brand-new light-up ones, her gift from Autry.

Marissa glanced in the hall mirror. No makeup. Her hair all messy. She smoothed it best she could and yanked down her long T-shirt over her black leggings. Well, if this was how she was going to look to tell Autry she loved him, so be it. This was who she was. A woman in flip-flops. Some things really would never change.

"Let's go, girls!"

Marissa pulled open the door.

Autry was standing there, his hand raised to knock.

She gasped. She looked at him, six feet plus of gorgeous, sexy Autry, a millionaire with a heart she'd never imagined such a man could have. Autry would give you the shirt off his back, even if he was pen-

niless and had nothing. She knew that. Autry would
soothe an upset child with the right words—not plati-
tudes or what he thought Marissa might want to hear
him say, but what a nine-year-old girl needed to know.
Autry bought school supplies and pencil-cap erasers in
animal shapes. And he made delicious spaghetti and
meatballs. He'd even sat through a handful of animated
movies. He was pure gold.

He stared at her, then smiled at the three little Fullers crowded behind her. "I have something to say to
you, Marissa."

She lifted her chin. "I have something to say to *you*."

Question was, should she go first and risk sound-
ing like a fool? He should go first. But what if he said
he'd only come to say a final goodbye, that she was
right that there was no future? Then she'd feel stupid
for telling him she loved him.

She should go first. She should say how she felt,
no matter what. That was what she would teach her
girls. To speak their truth. To risk. To put themselves
out there.

"You first," he said.

Oh God.

Autry stood on the porch, waiting to hear what Marissa had to say. Goodbye, he figured. And he wasn't
ready to hear it. His plane wasn't leaving for hours. He
had time to prolong his agony. But at least he'd be in
agony while looking at Marissa's beautiful face.

"But first," he said, "where were you all going in
such a hurry?" He smiled at three-year-old Kaylee,
who was still in her pajamas.

"Look, Mr. Autry," Kaylee said and she stomped

the porch, her sneakers lighting up. "Thank you for my sneakers. Thank you for being so nice."

Autry knelt down. "Thank you for your being such a great three-year-old." He pulled her into a hug.

Kiera pushed past her mom's leg. "Thanks for my new backpack," she said, tears glistening. "And my monkey key ring."

"You're very welcome, Kiera." He wrapped her in a hug.

Abby stepped forward. "I'm not going to cry. I made myself a promise, so that I wouldn't ruin the goodbye by being a blubbering mess."

Autry laughed. "You can cry. I'm going to cry."

"You cry?" Kaylee asked. "But you're a grown-up."

"Well, sometimes grown-ups cry when they get really sad. And leaving you guys, well, that makes me really sad."

"But you have to," Abby said. "Because you're going to Paris."

He nodded. "I am going to Paris. In just several hours. But where were you guys headed just now?" He realized he'd never gotten an answer to that question.

Marissa crossed her arms over her chest. In a protective gesture? "To find you."

"Why?"

She glanced at her daughters, who were all staring at her. *Well, go ahead. Say it. Speak your truth.*

"Because I love you, Autry Jones. And I couldn't let you go without telling you."

She felt her daughters staring at her. Out of the corner of her eye she could see their mouths hanging open, then glee light their faces.

"You love me?" he asked.

"I love you," she said. "I didn't think I had any room left in my heart. But I was wrong."

Kaylee stepped forward. "I love Autry, too. He's really nice. He makes really good steaks. And I love my new backpack."

Kiera said, "I love you, Mr. Autry, because you're really good at charades."

"I guess it's my turn to tell Autry that I love him and say why," Abby said. "But I'm keeping it my own special secret. Is that okay?"

Autry knelt in front of Abby. "Of course it's okay. But one of the reasons I came here this morning was to tell you that you were right."

Abby tilted her head. "Me? Right about what?"

"Remember when you sang me your own version of 'Only You'?"

"Of course," Abby said, glancing at him with half shyness, half anticipation.

"You were right that only I can be your new dad," Autry said.

Four gasps filled the air.

"And your dad, and your dad," he said to Kaylee and Kiera. He stood up and looked at Marissa, taking her hand. "I love you, too, Marissa. I love you with everything I am. I love all of you."

"Oh, Autry," Marissa said, and launched herself into his arms.

Their audience cheered and clapped.

"But you're leaving tonight! You're going to Paris."

"Not if I'm going alone," he said. "Not without the four Fullers who've become my family."

She stared at him. "What? What do you mean?"

Autry held her gaze and reached out a hand to touch

her beautiful face. "Come with me. All of you. Come to Paris."

"What?" she said again, her head spinning.

"This morning I ran into Travis Dalton and Brenna O'Reilly. I hadn't had a chance to meet them before, so it was nice that I got to before I left. Travis said something that really got to me."

"Oh my God, you met Travis!" Abby squealed. "I knew him before he was famous, but you met him after. How cool is that?"

Marissa ruffled Abby's hair with a smile, then turned to Autry. "What did Travis say?"

"He said, 'If you want this woman, then go get her. If you can walk away, then do that. That's how you'll know.'"

"Huh," Marissa said with a grin. "I wouldn't have taken Travis for a love guru, but I guess Brenna has changed him."

"I can't walk away from you, Marissa. Or from your daughters. I love you. But yes, I'm going to Paris for a year, maybe longer. I want you and the girls to come with me. Not today, of course—I'm assuming none of you have passports and you'll need to apply and wait for them to arrive. Then we'll need to look into schools and a bigger home than the one I'm renting for the year. Oh, and of course the Raffertys are welcome to come, if they'd like."

Marissa looked slightly dazed and he smiled. "But... but we don't speak French," she stammered.

"We do!" Abby said. "We know *bonjour* and *adieu* and the other word for goodbye!"

"Au revoir," Autry said. "Don't make me say it for real."

"We want Paris! We want Paris!" all three girls started chanting.

He watched Marissa's face. He could see the emotions racing across. Excitement. Fear. Hope. And the word *but*. He saw the word *but*.

"I need to think," she said. "Excuse me for a moment. Girls, will you stay out here with Mr. Autry?"

His heart plummeted. She was going inside to have the space to think, without the girls' hopeful faces. Without his hopeful face.

She was going to come out and tell him no.

Marissa closed the door behind her, her eyes wide like saucers, her heart beating like mad.

Was she going to uproot her daughters? Herself? Change her entire life to move to Paris?

Yes, dammit. She was. Hadn't she said that today was the first day of the rest of her life? Hell yeah, she had.

She was doing this. Small-town gal Marissa Fuller was moving to Paris with her daughters to be with the man she loved. The father they all loved. And they were going to be a family.

Except... Wait.

She frowned, biting her lip. He hadn't said anything about marriage.

She wasn't uprooting her children and moving to a foreign country without a ring on her finger, that was for sure. No commitment, no France.

Her chin lifted, she opened the door and stepped back outside. Her daughters were staring at her. Abby was biting her lips so hard Marissa was afraid she might draw blood, and the girl's hands were in prayer formation.

Autry smiled—that captivating smile that always made her knees weak. "It's four against one, Marissa. You're outnumbered and overruled."

"Oh, wow," Abby said, jumping up and down. "I just realized I'll get to be a bridesmaid at my own mother's wedding!"

Marissa felt her cheeks burn. Well, at least the subject had come up! "Honey, Autry didn't say anything about us getting married. He just invited us to move to Paris with him."

And told her daughters he was their new father. He wouldn't have said that unless—

"I didn't say anything about marriage?" Autry asked. "Well, of course I didn't. How could I say anything about marriage without getting down on one knee?" He did just that and took a small velvet box out of his pocket.

Marissa gasped for the tenth time that morning. So did the girls.

"Marissa Fuller, will you do me the honor of becoming my wife?" he asked, opening the box to reveal a gleaming, twinkling diamond.

"That is some rock!" Abby shrieked.

Marissa's eyes widened. A certain little girl was growing up way too fast. Either Abby was listening in on Grandma's viewing of her guilty-pleasure TV show, *Real Housewives*, or the gals at Bee's Beauty Parlor forgot themselves when little ears were around. She smiled at Autry.

Then it hit her. The man had just proposed to her!

"Oh, Autry," she said, unable to say anything else,

unable to speak. The air had whooshed out of her body. She took a breath and looked at the man she loved so much. "Yes!" she shouted. "Yes, yes, yes! I will marry you!"

Autry stood up and slid the beautiful diamond ring on her finger.

She was so overwhelmed for a moment that she covered her mouth with her hand, then turned to her daughters. "Girls, we're moving to Paris!"

"Today?" Kiera asked, clapping.

"Not today," Marissa explained. "When you go to another country, you have to have something called a passport. So we have to get those and make arrangements. But in about a month, we'll be joining Autry in Paris."

"Yay!" Abby shrieked. "This is more exciting than if Lyle rejoined 2LOVEU! Oh, and you two can get married at the Eiffel Tower!"

"Or here," Autry said. "Whatever would make my bride-to-be happy. If you want to get married at the Ace in the Hole, that would be fine with me."

Marissa laughed. She couldn't see Autry Jones saying I do beside the pool table and dartboard. Or maybe she could. He'd changed. She'd changed. And now all their lives were changing.

"I don't care where we get married as long as we do," he said. "And I want us to become a family as soon as possible." He pulled Marissa into his arms. "I love you."

"I love *you*."

"A kiss to seal the deal?" he asked Marissa.

The girls giggled. "Ooh, la, la," Abby said.

Autry took her face in his hands and kissed her so passionately that she felt her toes curl.

"Bonjour!" Kiera said and they all cracked up. Out of the mouths of babes.

As Marissa gazed into the gorgeous blue eyes of her fiancé, she vaguely heard her daughters planning a Euro Disney wedding with Mickey Mouse as the officiant. The future was theirs—as a family.

Epilogue

Autry took a photo of Marissa and the girls sitting on the low stone wall along the Seine, Abby holding the baguette they'd just bought from a café.

"We're in Paris. I still can't believe it," Marissa said, touching the charming, very Parisian silk scarf she'd purchased from a little boutique. Her daughters already looked like French schoolgirls. They had started at the American school last week and were fitting in well. All three were enchanted with Paris, and Abby and Janie were texting away, sharing photos of home and France.

A few months from now, she and Autry would say "I do." Nope, not in Paris, their adopted city. In Rust Creek Falls, in the Ace in the Hole, where they'd met. Where a man who didn't date single mothers first fell for a single mom. And where a widowed mother of three who didn't think she'd ever find love again, found it.

Marissa's phone beeped with a text. Her mom and dad texting their first selfie at the railing of the *Caribbean*

Star cruise ship. Her mother's big smile and her dad's rested expression made Marissa so happy.

"I love you, Marissa," Autry said, standing behind her and wrapping his arms around her.

"I love you, too," she said.

"Je t'aime aussi!" Kaylee said.

Marissa and Autry stared at the little girl, their mouths agape.

Marissa turned to Autry. "Did my three-year-old just say 'I love you, too' in French?"

"She most definitely did," Autry said, picking up Kaylee and kissing her on the cheek.

"Ooh, la, la," Kiera said. It had become one of her favorite phrases. *"Je t'aime, je t'aime!"* She twirled around and Autry picked her up with his other arm, two little Fullers caught for hugs.

Just then, a little stray dog came and swiped the baguette right out of Abby's hand and ran off.

"There are many more where that baguette came from," Autry said.

Marissa laughed. "To Paris. And to us."

"To all of us," Autry said, as Abby came rushing over for the family hug.

* * * * *

SPECIAL EXCERPT FROM

H HARLEQUIN®

SPECIAL EDITION

Rancher Zach Dalton places a classified ad searching for the perfect wife—but instead finds the perfectly imperfect Lydia Grant. She may not be everything he wants, but she could be just what this cowboy needs!

Read on for a sneak preview of the next book in the MONTANA MAVERICKS: THE GREAT FAMILY ROUNDUP continuity, **THE MAVERICK'S BRIDE-TO-ORDER** *by USA TODAY bestselling author* **Stella Bagwell**.

"Lydia Grant, assistant manager," he read, then lifted a questioning glance to her. "Is that you?"

Her head made a quick bob, causing several curls to plop onto her forehead. "That's me. Assistant manager is just one of my roles at the *Gazette*. I do everything around here. Including plumbing repair. You need a faucet installed?"

"Uh, no. I need a wife."

The announcement clearly took her aback. "I thought I misheard you earlier. I guess I didn't."

Enjoying the look of dismay on her face, he gave her a lopsided grin. "Nope. You didn't hear wrong. I want to advertise for a wife."

Rolling the pencil between her palms, she eyed him with open speculation.

"What's the matter?" she asked. "You can't get a wife the traditional way?"

As soon as Zach had made the decision to advertise for a bride, he'd expected to get this sort of reaction. He'd just not expected it from a complete stranger. And a woman, at that.

"Sometimes it's good to break from tradition. And I'm in a hurry."

Something like disgust flickered in her eyes before she dropped her gaze to the scratch pad in front of her. "I see. You're a man in a hurry. So give me your name, mailing address and phone number and I'll help you speed up this process."

She took down the basic information, then asked, "How do you want this worded? I suppose you do have requirements for your…bride?"

He drew up a nearby plastic chair and eased his long frame onto the seat. "Sure. I have a few. Where would you like to start?"

She looked up at him and chuckled as though she found their whole exchange ridiculous. Zach tried not to bristle. Maybe she didn't think any of this was serious. But sooner or later Lydia Grant, and every citizen in Rust Creek Falls, would learn he was very serious about his search for a wife.

Don't miss
THE MAVERICK'S BRIDE-TO-ORDER
by Stella Bagwell, available September 2017 wherever
Harlequin® Special Edition books and ebooks are sold.

www.Harlequin.com

LOVE
Harlequin
romance?

Join our Harlequin community to share your thoughts and connect with other romance readers!

Be the first to find out about promotions, news, and exclusive content!

Sign up for the Harlequin e-newsletter and download a free book from any series at

www.TryHarlequin.com

CONNECT WITH US AT:

Harlequin.com/Community

Facebook.com/HarlequinBooks

Twitter.com/HarlequinBooks

Instagram.com/HarlequinBooks

Pinterest.com/HarlequinBooks

ReaderService.com

**ROMANCE WHEN
YOU NEED IT**

HSOCIAL2017

Reward the book lover in you!

Earn points from all your Harlequin book purchases from wherever you shop.

Turn your points into *FREE BOOKS* of your choice
OR
EXCLUSIVE GIFTS from your favorite authors or series.

Join for FREE today at
www.HarlequinMyRewards.com.

Harlequin My Rewards is a free program (no fees) without any commitments or obligations.

MYR17